SHADOW VALLEY

SHADOW VALLEY

Barry Cord

CHIVERS
THORNDIKE

This Large Print edition is published by BBC Audiobooks Ltd, Bath, England and by Thorndike Press®, Waterville, Maine, USA.

Published in 2004 in the U.K. by arrangement with Golden West Literary Agency.

Published in 2004 in the U.S. by arrangement with Golden West Literary Agency.

U.K. Hardcover   ISBN 0–7540–9986–5 (Chivers Large Print)
U.K. Softcover   ISBN 0–7540–9987–3 (Camden Large Print)
U.S. Softcover   ISBN 0–7862–6309–1 (Nightingale)

The text of this Large Print edition is unabridged.
Other aspects of the book may vary from the original edition.

Set in 16 pt. New Times Roman.

Printed in Great Britain on acid-free paper.

British Library Cataloguing in Publication Data available

Library of Congress Control Number: 2003116423

CHAPTER ONE

Cole Barrett came through Cibola Pass at sundown, and his first impression of Shadow Valley was one of peace. The ragged peaks of the Conquistadores were at his back, casting their long shadows across the wide valley below, and they were like a company of ghostly cavalry marching across the mesa-broken land.

Somewhere in the dimming distance mission bells were calling the faithful to vespers.

This was the way Cole first saw Shadow Valley, and it did not jibe with what he knew. Why here? he thought sourly. What brought my father here?

He had no answers for his questions.

He shifted his weight in the saddle, letting his legs support the burden for a while. He was dog-tired. He had been riding hard since he had left Fort Benton more than a week ago and he still wore his cavalryman's uniform without insignia and tunic, although he no longer was a member of the U. S. Army. This was Texas, the year 1870—and that uniform was still a challenge in the sullen Lone Star state. But Cole Barrett wore his campaign hat tipped at an insolent angle, as an outward symbol of his defiance of the country through which he was riding.

1

He let his bay have its blow while his gaze ranged the land below him. Hemmed in on the north and west by the savage Conquistadores and on the east by the Pinnacles, the valley was pretty much insulated to settlers from those directions. Only from the south was travel easy, and for that reason Shadow Valley had remained predominantly Mexican long after the territory itself had become Texan.

An old Mexican road came through here, joining the more traveled artery to Santa Fe beyond the hills. This was the Aragon road through Cibola Pass, and Cole, coming in from the north, was the first rider in almost a decade to take this historic line of travel into the valley. Down past the first sharp bend of this *camino* an adobe structure shouldered outward from the sandstone cliff, and Cole, laying his tired glance on it, wondered briefly: Maybe they'll know where the Cross B is located.

He had come far for this, but now that he was here a growing doubt began to check his urgency. He would not have come at all, he reflected, if his father had not written. In seven years Marcus Barrett's note had been the only communication he had received from his parents and it had burned itself in his mind.

Dear Son:
Your mother died yesterday. I promised her I would write you. I been meaning to

2

for a long time, but I've been a stubborn fool. I need you. If you can come, come at once. Jay's dead. Billy's gone wild. Barney ain't the same man you knew. And Martha's strange. I got a fight on my hands here and nobody I can depend on. I'll be waiting for you.

It had taken his father seven years to break his silence, to bridge the gap of a long misunderstanding. Cole remembered that he had made the first move toward reconciliation right after Appomattox. He had ridden back to the old Barrett ranch on the Brazos, only to find his family gone.

'Headed west,' a neighbor informed him, eyeing Cole's uniform with hostility. 'Somewhere west of the Pecos.'

Cole had drifted around a bit after that and wound up back in the Army. He was stationed at Fort Benton when his father's letter, addressed in care of the Army postmaster, had reached him.

How's it gonna be? he thought with sudden restlessness. How will it be in the new place?

Then his old anger stirred and he shrugged his shoulders. He knew he would not take anything from his father or his brothers—they'd have to take him as he was or the devil with them! He had always been a little apart from the rest of the family, both physically and in his ways of thinking. He would not bend to

3

his father's stern will—and a break had been inevitable.

It had come when he was eighteen.

Of that scene he remembered now only his mother's white face. And with that remembrance came a sudden sorrow that he would never see her again, that she would never again come to him, as in the brown days of his angry boyhood, to ease his bitterness with words of understanding.

The bay lifted its head, and Cole said: 'We'll be home tonight, Omar.' But the words fell flat on his ears and he wondered what had brought the Barretts to this hemmed-in valley so close to the Mexican border.

It was two miles down to the adobe structure on the valley trail, and daylight was soft and without brilliance when he drew up by the door.

A huge bull's head was mounted above the heavy weathered portal. It was not that of the longhorn breed, but of a Muerra bull. The sleek dark head of the vicious strain raised for fighting in the bull rings of Mexico City. A brass ring was set in the broad nose, and from the ring a brass chain supported a weathered board sign: El Toro.

Three horses nosed the tiepole to the left of the door, shaded by an oak that was more than a century old. From inside the inn came sounds of merriment, drawing toward the entrance, and a man's voice, strong and clear,

4

singing a ribald version of 'Johnny Reb.'

Some warning roused Cole. He turned the bay in toward the others, his glance picking up the brand on the nearest cayuse's hip. A thin straight line with a saber handle.

The door swung open then and men came down into the twilight. The singer was leading. Cole swung around in the saddle and faced him, laying his cool glance on a freckled face under an off-center Stetson. Nineteen, he judged. Built like an ox. Thick solid torso, heavy arms and shoulders. A sixgun snugged in a holster, tied down to his right thigh.

He was holding a whiskey bottle in his hand as he came around the weathered tierack, and he saw Cole watching him just as the tall, sour-faced man behind him suddenly stopped and said sharply: 'Calico!'

The freckled youngster dropped the whiskey bottle. He stood rigid, fear in his widening eyes. Then the last man, coming down behind them, sneered: 'Yore eyesight's bad, Monte. That ain't Calico. Not in them pants!'

He came on down the steps, pushing Monte aside. He was a tall, heavy-boned man of about forty-five, and Cole saw his face, hatchet-sharp and sandy-stubbled under his dusty Stetson. Pale gray eyes touched Cole lightly, like the flick of light off a carbine barrel, and then moved on to the youngster still standing spraddle-legged at the head of the rack.

Laughter roughened the man's voice.

'The soljer frighten yuh, Mike?'

The words stung. The liquor flush came back to the youngster's face till it almost matched the dusty red of his neckerchief. The man behind him, thin and long-armed and malevolently spiteful, added fuel to the kid's rage. 'Sing him another stanza, Mike. Mebbe he'd like to hear it.'

Mike moved away from the tierack and Cole saw what was coming. For an instant his eyes lay on the other two—Monte and the sandy-bearded man who had egged the kid on. They're not in on this, he thought coolly. They just want to see the kid rough me up. They'll stay clear—maybe.

Then Mike was up close, solid and belligerent, and Cole's temper quickened. The kid planted himself solidly, his voice tough. 'Kinda out of your territory, ain't yuh, yellowleg?'

Cole slid his left foot over the saddle horn and turned so that he sat in the swell of his saddle, facing the man below. His body hung loose and pliant while he judged distances. Past Mike the other two were shadowy, waiting figures.

'Not particularly,' he drawled.

Mike wagged his head on his bull neck. He was evidently a hardcase youngster who probably had roughed up men bigger and older than himself. An arrogant youngster,

6

physically sure of himself, and inclined to cockiness. As such he had a reputation to uphold, and this he intended to do for the benefit of the men at his back.

'Never ran into a Union cavalryman that wasn't as yeller as his neckerchief. You gonna get down, or will I have to yank yuh off?'

'That's big talk, kid,' Cole said dryly. 'Don't try something you won't be able to handle.'

Mike grunted. He stepped forward and shot out a hand for Cole's left boot. Cole snapped his right leg out. His toe caught Mike under the chin, snapping his head up. The kid staggered back and Cole slid out of saddle. He jammed his palm into Mike's face before the kid recovered, and Mike sat down heavily.

The shock jarred him. He sat dazed for a brief moment; then humiliation cleared his numbed brain. He scrambled up, his fingers reaching for his gun.

Cole wasted no energy. He wanted to end this fast and in a way that would imprint itself on the youngster's mind.

He stepped into Mike's rush, his Colt clearing leather in a swift, smooth motion. His body pivot was beyond the six-inch muzzle he jammed into Mike's stomach.

The wind whooshed out of Mike's lungs. His knees buckled. He started to collapse against Cole, the whites of his eyes showing in a suddenly lemon-yellow face.

Cole put a contemptuous hand on Mike's

7

right shoulder and pushed. The shove pivoted the other halfway around on rubbery legs and Cole booted him in the seat of his pants. The kick lifted Mike a foot off the ground and sent him sprawling into the dust by the tiebar, almost under the hind legs of a short-coupled sorrel.

It had happened fast and it caught Mike's companions flat-footed. Cole stood in the dust by his restive bay, his Army Colt backing his sharp challenge: 'You fellers backing the kid's play?'

The dour man shook his head and looked at his companion. The sandy-bearded hombre grinned. His thumb was hooked in his gunbelt, but there was no tension in him, nor apparent hostility. He said: 'Mike asked for it. You did a neat job, soljer.'

He came on then, chewing on the wad of his tobacco he had cuddled in his left cheek. He looked down at the writhing Mike, shrugged, spat into the dust. His eyes came up to meet Cole's.

'I don't know who you are,' he said. 'But I have a job for you at Saber any time you want it, hombre. Just ask for Cash Gillis.'

'I'll keep that in mind,' Cole said coldly.

Gillis grinned and turned to the sour-faced Monte. 'Give me a hand with him.' He started to bend over the sick youngster, then suddenly straightened and stepped away. 'Dang it!' he cursed mildly. 'All that good likker gone tuh blazes.'

Monte joined him and they dragged Mike to his feet. His legs wouldn't hold him. Cash swabbed the kid's mouth with Mike's dirty neckerchief. Then they walked him to a rangy black pony wedged in between the sorrel and a roan, both wearing Saber brands. Mike was beginning to come out of his nausea when his companions heaved him up into his saddle. Monte steadied him as he sagged and clutched for his saddle horn.

Cash Gillis stepped back and picked up the whiskey bottle Mike had dropped. His movements were as deceptively clumsy as the rolling slouch of a grizzly. He straightened and looked at Cole, a faint grin on his hard face. 'You look like Calico at that,' he admitted.

'Friend of yourn?' Cole asked shortly.

'Heck no!'

The Saber man walked back to his waiting companions and mounted his roan. Monte had unhitched the black and hooked the reins around Mike's saddle horn. Cash put a hand on the youngster's shoulder. 'Hold on, kid. You'll get to feelin' better when we reach the fork.'

They backed around and rode past Cole. Mike's eyes met his briefly, lighting up with a deep, intense hate. Then they were past, swinging sharply down the trail to the darkening valley, and Cole started abruptly, trying to fit what he had just noticed into a

9

pattern.

Both Monte and Cash Gillis were riding Saber cayuses. But Mike was in the saddle of a Cross B horse!

CHAPTER TWO

The anger ran out of Cole, leaving its residue of bitter tiredness. It was not the first time he had run into trouble wearing elements of the Union uniform. It was too soon after Appomattox, and Texas was still turbulently rebellious because of the mistakes of the Reconstruction. Cole knew he would always run into men like Mike.

The sun's afterglow was fading over the western curl of the Conquistadores, and for the first time that day Cole felt a breeze chill the sweat on his back. He holstered his Colt and unconsciously hitched at a saber that no longer hung from his waist.

The glassy eyes in the bull's head over the inn door caught the fading light and glinted mockingly as he turned toward it. He pushed his campaign hat back on his head, a gray and bitter distaste of what lay ahead suddenly flooding him.

The heavy door swung in easily under his hand and he passed through the low, oaken arch into a huge room built more than a

10

century before. There was a sense of massive permanence in the room, embodied in the solid, hand-rubbed walnut bar across the rear wall that was at variance with the flimsy board counters of his acquaintance. This place had been built by a people with a tradition, a bulwark on the Spanish road to an American empire.

Situated on the hill above Shadow Valley, on the Cibola road, its thick walls had provided sanctuary from Indian raiders out of the Conquistadores, and offered overnight lodgings for government officials traveling to the 'northern provinces' beyond the dangerous hills.

Time had changed the direction of empirical thrust and put the destiny of the country into another people's hands—the tall *Anglos* had opened a new way into the valley through the Pinnacles, and the old Cibola road had fallen into disuse. El Toro's had settled back to wait with an air of timeless patience, wrapped in an aura of old glories and memories of the days when satin-padded coaches escorted by armored, sword-belted guards had pulled up before its heavy door.

Some of this Cole felt, without knowing the details. And again the thought came to him, wonderingly: What are the Barretts doing here? What brought my father to this land?

The voice struck across his thoughts, soft and cultured and with veiled malice.

11

'Welcome, *señor*' to El Toro.'

Cole was just inside the door; the big room was lighted only by wax tapers in a three-pronged chandelier over the middle of the bar which barely lightened the middle shadows. The voice came from the gloom to his right, where the wall of the inn faced the long drop to the valley.

A window faced him as he turned and against it a dark shape was silhouetted in bulky outline. The words were a welcome, but something in the man's tone conveyed an enmity as unrelenting as it was unexpected. Cole felt the hair on his neck prickle his skin.

He realized suddenly that he was standing in the doorway, a fine target against the lightness of the sky behind him, and he stepped abruptly away, his hand dropping to the heel of his Army Colt.

'I'd feel more welcome,' he said bluntly, 'if I could see who was doing it?'

The watcher chuckled. 'You are a suspicious man, *señor*.' Wheels creaked thinly in the room and the shape moved against the window and formed out of the shadows.

Surprise hit Cole a sharp blow. He had not expected this—a man in a wheelchair!

The other halted on the borders of the dim light, his long fingers clamped around the iron-tired wheels. He was a tall man with broad deep shoulders, rounded now as he leaned forward over his blanket-swathed legs.

12

In his middle twenties, his Spanish ancestry was stamped in the proud hook of his thin nose, the olive shading of his skin. Pain had refined this man's ascetic features further, thinning them until his cheekbones were sharply prominent. Under dark, heavy eyebrow ridges his eyes had a luminous quality.

'A soldier, *señor*?' he asked politely, his lips smiling.

'No longer,' Cole replied. 'Just a stranger looking for a place to wash, eat, and,' he ran his fingers over the dark stubble of his jaw, 'a shave, perhaps?'

The man in the wheelchair nodded. 'My uncle, Carlos, will take care of you. For myself,' he indicated his blanketed legs, 'I can only offer you welcome.'

Cole nodded. He felt his hunger gnaw in his stomach and he turned to the bar. The invalid's eyes followed him.

'It's been many years, *señor*,' he pointed out, 'since anyone has come through the Conquistadores along the *Camino de Cibola*.'

'I was in a hurry,' Cole said shortly. Impatience began to crowd him. The man's questioning irritated him. 'I'd like to see yore uncle,' he said roughly.

'But of course,' the other replied quickly. He fumbled at the side of his chair for a hickory cane and thumped it on the plank floor.

An older man with a long sad face came to the doorway behind the bar. His shirtsleeves were rolled up to his hairy elbows. He stopped and looked at Cole, his eyes dark and unfriendly.

'Yes, *señor*?'

Cole came up to the bar, feeling an unhealthy atmosphere hang like a shroud over this dimly lighted room. He could not explain it, and he rejected it, pushing it out of his head.

'Tequila,' he ordered. He watched Carlos glance past him to his nephew before reaching for a bottle on the well-filled shelf behind him.

He waited while his glass was filled. Carlos pushed bottle and glass to him and Cole asked: 'I'm looking for the Cross B. You could save me a lot of useless riding if you'd point out the shortest way to the ranch.'

Carlos shrugged. 'The *camino* would have taken you to San Ramos,' he said slowly, 'and anyone in the village would have directed you.' He hesitated. 'Come,' he added quietly, moving around the long bar. 'I will show you.'

Cole followed him across the big room to the window where the invalid waited, staring with detached interest into the valley. Carlos put a hand on the back of the wheelchair and waited for Cole to come up.

'Sebastian likes to see the lights of San Ramos,' he explained. 'One can see them from here. See!'

Sebastian stirred and looked up into his uncle's face. Carlos shrugged. His voice had a sudden flat briskness. 'That *montana.*' He pointed. 'The sun is still on it. The peak shaped like the claw of a hammer.'

Cole nodded.

'There, where the shadow of Claw Mountain falls, you will find the Cross B rancho,' Carlos continued. 'Down the *camino* perhaps two miles you will find a trail that cuts across the broken country. It is not a good road, *señor,* but it will take you to the Cross B much sooner than along the San Ramos road.' He turned and studied Cole. 'Perhaps it is not for me to say—but if it is work you are looking for I would not advise the Cross B. There is a curse on the rancho—'

'I'm not looking for work, Carlos.'

Carlos shrugged resignedly. 'As you wish, *señor.*' He turned away from the window. 'You are hungry, perhaps —and you wish to wash and shave. *Si?*'

Cole nodded. 'An' my horse, Carlos—'

'He shall be attended to,' promised the innkeeper.

'If you will follow me,' Carlos said. He crossed the room with Cole behind him and they went up worn, creaking steps to a white-washed adobe hallway that gleamed a ghostly gray in the gloom. Carlos walked with the sureness of familiarity. Striking a match, he touched it to the candle sitting in a holder on a

15

heavy, hand-shaped chest pushed up against the wall. They went down the wide corridor.

'In here, *señor*,' Carlos said, pushing open a door. He walked to the bedstand, tilted the glass chimney of a china-based lamp and touched candle flame to the wick. He made a gesture with his free hand. 'This is my room. It will bring me pleasure if you will use my razor, *señor*. I will have *a muchacho* bring up more water.'

He went out, closing the door behind him.

Cole listened to his steps until they had faded into the silence that seemed an integral part of this ancient Spanish hostelry. He found water in a glazed earthen pitcher and soap in a wooden holder on the washstand. He washed himself, and as he toweled himself dry he looked into the ornate-framed mirror over the dresser.

The lamplight brought out the hollows in his face and his dark beard accentuated the harsh angle of his cheek-bones. It was a sensitive face hardened by living, but his brown eyes retained their even and detached humor that had so angered his father.

He had never resembled the Barretts, as his father had ragingly told him many times when he was a boy growing up on the Brazos ranch. He was dark and wiry where the Barretts were all heavy-boned and blond—they were six-footers all. Strong men physically and in their convictions. There had been Jay and Barney

16

and Bill—his brothers. And there was his sister Martha who looked like him.

A knock on the door turned him from the mirror. A fifteen-year-old Mexican youth in ragged *pantalones* came in, carrying a pitcher of hot water. He smiled vacantly at Cole as he set the water down on the dresser and looked at Cole a moment like an unwanted mongrel pup, his eyes shiny with interest, his tongue dumb. Cole dug two-bits out of his pocket and gave it to him, and the boy nodded vigorously, smiled again, and shuffled out of the room.

Cole shaved. The process seemed to take ten years from him. The quick clean lines of his face were youthful and pleasant—he was only twenty-six—but a fretting restlessness tightened his long thin lips. He was not a patient man by nature, but he had learned the value of patience in the Army and he kept his impulses under control now.

He dried Carlos' razor, thinking that tonight he'd see his father again after eight years—and he couldn't imagine how it would be.

He pushed the unsatisfying speculation out of his head and turned to the door. The sound of a rider coming at a clip along the valley trail held him. He turned and walked to the narrow casement window which looked down on the *camino*.

A slim rider in a broad Mexican sombrero passed under his window and turned in to the hitchrack. The rider dismounted and stood undecided, watching Cole's bay feeding from a bucket between its forelegs. The shadows did not permit a clear appraisal, but Cole knew the newcomer was a woman.

He eased back from the window, his hand reaching for his tobacco sack in an instinctive gesture. Rather late, he thought idly, for a woman to be riding . . .

He went out, turning down the dim hallway and finding the stairs. He stopped to put his cigarette into his mouth and light a match to it. The voices reached him as he started down . . .

'He came here, Sebastian! I know Julio—'

Sebastian's tone, sharp and dry, cut like a knife in the darkness below. 'You're a little fool, Juanita. How would I know what has happened to your brother?'

'He came here,' the girl repeated intensely. 'He told me. He said: "Juanita, I am riding to El Toro to see Sebastian about a very important matter. I do not expect to be gone long. But if I should not return tonight, ask Sebastian why." You see? That's what he said, and he was serious when he told me. That's why I've come, Sebastian.'

The invalid laughed. 'Julio always liked his little mysteries, even when we were boys and played together among the ruins under Castle Mesa.' His voice thinned, and suddenly a sharp and bitter hurt cut at the girl. 'What is there I can know of your brother's disappearance, Juanita? Have I perhaps something to do with

18

it? *Me—a cripple?*'

The girl's tone softened. 'I don't know, Sebastian. But I am worried—'

She turned as Cole's weight creaked on a loose step. For a moment her eyes flared wide, lighting to a flash of hope. She called out: 'Julio!' But she realized her mistake even as she called.

Cole paused at the foot of the stairs. The candlelight showed him Sebastian and the girl by the window, and his glance held on her a moment. She was standing by the wheelchair, her hands encased in soft yellow riding gloves which matched the mass of hair that lay in loose waves on her shoulders. There was an impatience in her. She moved away from Sebastian, a rather tall girl in charro jacket that couldn't conceal the soft curves beneath her white silk blouse. There was temper in her too, and Cole saw it in the way she held herself.

She's had her way with men all her life, Cole thought idly. She's too pretty—and too bossy.

He started to move away and her voice came out at him, sharp with annoyance. 'You startled me, *señor.* I do not like men who stop to listen in the dark.'

Irritation tugged at Cole's temper. 'Next time,' he said dryly, 'I'll fire a couple of shots into the air.' He turned his back on her and walked to the bar.

Behind him he heard Sebastian's low,

19

mocking laughter. 'The *estranjero* is a hard man, Juanita—you did not awe him. Don't be too harsh with him. He does not yet know the power of the Aragons. Nor the temper of Juanita—'

The girl turned like a lithe cat, her eyes luminous with a sudden anger, and she slapped Sebastian across the face with the back of her hand. 'Some day,' she flared, 'you will mock me once too often—'

Sebastian's hand reached out, his fingers clamping on her slim wrist. He pulled her to him in a rough gesture.

'It's been easy to forget,' he said. His voice was low, but there was pain in it and an ugly temper, and it told Cole, who had turned to watch, a lot of things.

The girl tried to pull away. 'Let me go—'

Sebastian laughed. 'Not until you—'

She slapped him again, a vicious cut across the cheek. Even in the poor light Cole noticed the white bloodless patch it left on Sebastian's face. And he saw the ugly stain of murder come up swiftly in the cripple's eyes.

The hand holding the girl's wrist tightened. It brought her up against the wheelchair in an involuntary move, her knees buckling to the pain of it. Sebastian's other hand went up swiftly, his fingers curling around her throat.

Cole came across the room then. It was none of his affair, but he wouldn't stand by and watch this. He took hold of Sebastian's arm and tried to pull it away from the girl's throat, and he realized instantly that he would never free her this way. He hated to do it, but he brought his left hand up in a hard smash against Sebastian's jaw.

The man's head jerked back against the chair and his grip relaxed. Cole caught the girl as she collapsed. The marks of Sebastian's fingers were still visible on her throat and her eyes had a glazed look. She gasped painfully, gulping in air.

He supported her almost dead weight, feeling her warmth in the curve of his arm, and it stirred memories and aroused pulsing restlessness in him. He picked her up and turned to the dining area where benches and tables made dim shapes. Her hair tickled his cheek with soft caress and his blood pounded in his ears and a sense of what he had missed was strong and dissatisfying in him.

She was breathing easier when he sat her down on a bench and went back to the bar for the tequila bottle still on the counter. He vaulted the bar and found a clean glass and came back to her, carrying both.

He poured half a tumbler of tequila and held it out to her. 'It'll help,' he said gently.

She took a sip and closed her eyes, her fingers reaching up to feel her throat. When she opened her eyes again Cole saw the shaken anger in her.

'The fool!' She sat up straight and looked

up into Cole's face. He was standing with the bottle in his hand, a lean and hard-faced man, faintly amused. Somehow his expression irked her. Juanita Aragon was not used to indifference in men.

She smiled archly. 'You are a capable man, *señor*. I thank you.'

Cole felt the purr in her voice. His glance reached out to Sebastian still slumped in his wheelchair. The pattern of the thing was plain—and he felt a sudden contempt for this girl who had pulled him into this affair.

'I'm sorry I had to hit him,' he said roughly. He hefted the bottle in his hand and turned, pushing his hat back on his head. He could almost feel the rage in the girl behind him.

Carlos parted the curtains to the kitchen behind the bar as Cole breasted the counter. The innkeeper came through, holding a tray before him. He looked tired and the scene did not immediately shape up for him. He said: 'I hope I haven't kept the *señor* waiting too long.'

'I was being entertained,' Cole said, indicating the girl.

Carlos' glance went past him to the girl getting up from the bench. 'Juanita!' His voice held sharp surprise.

'You were busy,' the girl explained. She came toward them, her features composed. She made a short gesture in the direction of the wheelchair. 'It would be well if you tended to Sebastian,' she said. 'He lost his head and

22

the soldier had to hit him, Carlos.'

'Hit him?' Carlos placed the tray on the bar and walked swiftly around the counter to his nephew. Sebastian stirred as he approached. His dark eyes touched his uncle and slid away, searching for Cole. He didn't say anything. He pushed himself up in his chair, his long fingers curling tightly around the chair sides.

Carlos hesitated, looking from Sebastian to the girl. 'What has happened?' he asked in some bewilderment. 'What could have caused this trouble?'

'It was nothing, Uncle,' Sebastian said sharply. 'I lost my head. The soldier did what he had to do.'

The apology in his voice brought the girl to him. She put a hand on his shoulder. 'I'm sorry, Sebastian. I was angry and worried about Julio. And my temper—'

'Is well known in the valley,' Sebastian finished coldly. He touched his jaw and turned to Cole, his eyes holding an ugly light. 'You see, *señor*,' he added with bitter amusement, 'it is not well to cross the Aragons.'

Carlos threw up his hands. 'I do not understand all this.'

Juanita smiled. 'Do not worry your head about it, Carlos. Sebastian and I quarreled—and the *Americano* intervened.' She shrugged. 'It is of no importance.'

Carlos shook his head. 'Something very important must have happened to bring you

23

here at this hour, *chiquita*. Already it is too late to travel safely back to your father's hacienda.'

'Not too late, Carlos,' the girl replied. 'I am not afraid of the night. As for my being here,' she turned her glance to Sebastian, 'I came looking for my brother. Julio has not been home in three days. Father is worried. Mother has taken to bed—'

'I am sorry to hear that,' Carlos said. 'Julio was here, yes.' He turned to his nephew. 'He came to see you, did he not? I remember he went with you into your room—'

'And he left,' Sebastian snapped. 'I assure you,' he turned to Juanita, 'I do not know the whereabouts of your brother. He may have run into someone from the gringo ranch, the Cross B.'

Carlos added grimly: 'You should know that it is hardly safe to ride in Shadow Valley, Juanita. Even now I am afraid for you.' He made a little gesture toward the window where a band of silver light was shining through. 'Look—the moon is full tonight.'

The girl gave a nervous laugh. 'I am mounted on the fastest horse in the valley, Carlos. No one will catch me tonight.' She put a hand on his arm, her voice friendly and somewhat apologetic. 'I am sorry I caused trouble, Carlos.' She turned and looked at Cole, her eyes cool and appraising. 'As for you, *señor*, I wish to thank you again. You are a brusque gentleman, but quite capable, and my father could use a man like you. If you have come to Shadow Valley looking for work, come to the Aragon rancho. My father will most certainly hire you.'

A funny little chuckle sounded in Cole's thoughts. This was his second offer of a job, from two different ranches, within the first hour of his arrival in the valley. He nodded gravely. 'I promise to consider it, ma'am.'

Sebastian's rocking laughter rustled through the room. He was leaning back, his eyes half closed, like a man enjoying a secret joke.

Temper showed briefly in Juanita's eyes, but this time it was controlled. She straightened her hat on her long golden hair.

Carlos said wearily: *'Buenas noches*, Juanita,' and walked with her to the door. He stood in the band of moonlight that came inside, an old and worried man, until the sound of her horse turning into the trail beat up against the night and faded away.

Then he turned, closed the door, and came back into the room. *'Por dios, señor,'* he said, suddenly remembering. 'I have forgotten your supper.'

Cole ate unhurriedly. Sebastian had wheeled himself around to the window again and was a silent shadow, staring moodily down into the well of blackness that was Shadow Valley. Carlos had gone back into the kitchen.

A sense of frustration lay in the room, as if

25

the bitterness of old Spain were somehow impregnated into the very adobe and wood of this old inn that had seen much of the pomp and the glory of the Conquistadores. Down in that valley that had been Spanish for more than one hundred years was the Cross B, an alien element. A faint premonition of what his father was up against came to Cole.

He pushed his plate aside and rolled himself a cigarette. Carlos came out of the kitchen and Cole rose, impatience suddenly nagging him to get moving.

'Come again, *señor*,' Carlos said as he paid his bill. Cole nodded and turned away. He was almost at the door when Sebastian said, without turning around:

'Yes, *Señor* Barrett. Come again.'

It stopped Cole and swung him sharply around. This brooding invalid knew who he was—*had known all along!*

Cole took in an angry breath.

Sebastian was still staring down into the valley, seemingly unaware of the reaction his words had produced. Carlos was staring at Cole from behind the counter, the lines in his face accentuated by the candlelight. The big room was silent and weighted with some unexplainable frustration.

A bitter distaste checked the angry confusion in Cole Barrett. He turned on his heel and went out.

CHAPTER THREE

The moon flooded the sandy trail with light and shadow, painting the chaparral with silver. Ahead of Cole was the town he had seen from El Toro's, but the Cross B, as pointed out by Carlos, lay to the west. The hills seemed far and remote and not quite real under the light of the climbing moon, and the claw-shaped peak seemed to hang by itself against the star-studded horizon.

The night air grew chill. Cole stopped and reached behind into his slicker roll for his brush jacket. The bay snorted wearily.

'Reckon yo're right, Omar,' Cole muttered. 'Ain't no sense riding in on the folks in the middle of the night.'

The long hard push across the Conquistadores had taken its toll of him. He felt suddenly bone-weary and his eyes began to close. Consequently, when the bay dipped down into a flat behind a cow-backed hill, he halted and made camp.

He built a small fire, after picketing Omar in the brush beyond, and sat with his back against his saddle, staring into the flames. Tomorrow he'd ride into the ranchyard of the new Cross B. Unconsciously he brushed a hand down along the yellow stripe of his dusty blue pants. What would his father say, knowing he had fought through four long and bitter years with Union cavalry?

He leaned back and looked up at the stars. The heat was going out of the valley, funneling through a pass in the Conquistadores. Somewhere a coyote yelped sharply, with hungry loneliness, and he felt it echoed in his heart. He had come back to his father's house because he had found nothing else to tie himself to, and because he was tired of drifting.

Omar stamped restlessly in the shadows of the mesquite tree. Cole stretched, tossing his cigarette into the embers. Just before he turned in he thought of Juanita Aragon and of the bitter loneliness of Sebastian . . .

*   *   *

Ten miles southeast of where Cole slept a tall man rode a magnificent palomino horse out of the deep shadows of a bald-topped hill. The horse was a Barb-Arabian! The man wore armor!

His chest plates reflected the moonlight. An inlaid silver-handled sword glinted at his right side. He wore a plumed hat. His face was hidden by a black mask that covered his eyes and nose. He was a sinister, disquieting figure in the night.

The palomino minced restively, eager to be on the move. The silent figure stretched out a gloved hand and stroked the yellow mane. Behind him, over the dark side, the moon was a swollen orb, still faintly orange.

'*Vamonos*,' the swordsman said grimly, and smiled as the palomino tossed its head. He reached behind him into his cantle pack and drew out a wine-velvet cloak. He put it on not because he was cold, but to hide the tell-tale glint of his armor.

'*Vamonos!*' he repeated, and his armor clinked against the moonlight night as the palomino whirled with an eager whinny and broke into a run for the San Ramos trail off to the west . . .

Along that trail Bill Barrett, blond and tough and hazily drunk, swayed in the saddle of a jogging gray mare. He had been due back at the Cross B before sundown, having been sent to San Ramos to hire desperately needed men for the roundup his brother Barney was conducting off the benches of the Pinnacles. He was returning empty-handed, to face his father's contempt and his sister's sharp tongue. All his life he had been forced to submit to the first, and he took the second only because he understood Martha and felt sorry for her.

He had spent a futile three hours in the Longhorn Saloon, trying to induce several hardcases to earn an honest living punching cattle, and had almost lost his temper and gotten into an argument with Buck Gaines, the town marshal.

Barney was up in the Breaks now, waiting for him to show up, trying to round up three thousand head with the help of four men and a Mex cook.

Billy shook his head. Liquor usually made him gay, but this night he felt morose. The trail reeled drunkenly ahead of him. Good thing the gray knows the way home, he thought. But he didn't really care if he got home or not. 'The devil with it!' he said aloud.

He was only twenty, but he had always been wild. He had been too young to get into the fight between the States, and he grew up in its aftermath. He grew up in the confusion that followed and it had influenced him. It seemed that the things he wanted to do he never did; either his father or his sister overrode him. He had developed into a big, likable chap, but this was a front covering a deep inner frustration. Morally he was weak—and he had to drink to hide that weakness from himself.

He swayed and caught at his saddle horn. It was that last drink at the Longhorn, he thought vaguely. Shouldn't have taken that last one.

The Cross B was shot to smithereens. Everyone knew it. No use trying to hold out now. 'I'm going to tell Paw,' he said aloud. 'The Cross B's shot an' finished.'

His voice sounded thick and distant to his ears. The world of lights and shadows seemed unreal.

30

Sure, he reflected dismally. Sell out! Bull Harkness, who ran the Longhorn Bar in San Ramos, was willing to buy. He had mentioned it again tonight. The price was an insult. But what else was there?

As far as he, Bill Barrett, was concerned, he was through. Through sweating it out against long odds. Riding fifteen hours a day—doing the work of two men. What for? He wasn't any good anyway. Didn't she tell him that? And her only a greaser!

He caught himself at that. Even drunk he respected her. Juanita Aragon. The most beautiful woman he had ever seen, the woman he had lost his heart to.

He hated the Aragons, every sneering, proud-faced son of them! They thought they owned the valley because they were here when Mexico was a Spanish colony . . .

The gray snorted in sudden alarm and stopped, its flanks quivering. Bill ran his palm across his eyes to clear them. The trail here crossed a wide sandy arroyo. The pale stream bed gleamed in the moonlight. The shadows were black among the thickets on the other side.

'Whassamatter?' he queried thickly. 'Don't you know the way home any more, muttonhead?'

The gray balked. Impatience surged through young Barrett. 'Dang it!' he shouted unreasonably. 'Get movin'!' He backed the command with a rake of spurs across the animal's withers. The gray jumped, scrambled down the crumbly bank.

The shadows moved on the trail ahead. A rider loomed out of the darkness and paused—a strange, cloaked rider mounted on a magnificent palomino horse.

For a numbed moment Bill stared at that somber shadow. Then fear acted like a douse of ice water, shocking him into startled soberness.

He clawed for his hip gun as the cloaked figure charged. The gray reared, frightened by the spectral figure. The abrupt move nearly unseated young Barrett. His hand fumbled at his holster.

The palomino plunged past. Bill Barrett had one instant of clarity before his destiny caught up with him. He saw the sword glint in its vicious arc toward him and instinctively he threw up his left arm to shield his face.

The razor-keen Toledo blade crunched through muscle and bone and was slowed enough so that it slashed his throat instead of entirely decapitating him. Blood spurted from arm and jugular. The fingers of Bill's right hand tightened convulsively over his holster gun and one of them pulled the trigger. The bullet smashed through his holster, raked down across his thigh and buried itself in the sand.

The shot absorbed the sound of the pivoting

palomino. It whirled on a dime, kicking up a spume of sand. Again the swordsman cut down with the glinting blade.

The gray staggered and went down on crumbling forelegs, its blood spilling out onto the cold sand. It keeled over on its side with Bill Barrett still in saddle. Pinned under the animal's weight, the Cross B man struggled convulsively, blindly, for a few silent moments.

The cloaked swordsman stood over him, bloody blade held before him in a grim gesture of salute. Then he carefully wiped the blade in the sand and scabbarded it. Bill Barrett was dead when he rode the palomino back up the long trail. The moon was settling in the mists in the west . . .

CHAPTER FOUR

The sun was up over the eastern rim when Cole Barrett rode down a dry wash and hit a well-defined trail running toward the claw-shaped butte. He had saddled and broken camp without eating, knowing he would be at his father's house before noon.

A steer lumbered out of a thicket of prickly pear and crossed his path, turning to stare at him as he passed. The Cross B brand faced him boldly from the animal's flank and he knew he was on his father's range.

The road curved away from an arroyo and then dipped down into it, merging with another that came up from the south. As he rode up to the junction a coyote appeared on the far bank, paused a moment to look at him, then streaked off. A moment later a pair of ugly buzzards flapped awkwardly into the sky, their broad wings beating heavily against the morning heat.

Cole reined in on the lip of the arroyo, his eyes narrowing on the blob in the middle of the sandy bed. The strengthening light washed down over the alkali bottom and a gluttony scavenger stared beadily at Cole, unwilling to leave the carcasses.

The horse lay on its side, its rigid legs testifying death had not been recent. A man lay crumbled under the still barrel, his head and shoulders and one leg showing.

A wave of revulsion shocked through Cole as the buzzard gave ground slowly. His hand jerked downward and came up with a gun nestling in his palm. His first shot tore the scavenger's head off, his second and third ripped into the ugly, twitching carcass.

He reloaded automatically, letting his gorge settle before he rode down to the beak-torn horse. It was a rangy gray with a blaze face and its throat had been slashed.

The man lay with his face buried in the sand, one arm outstretched, the stiff fingers still clutching a Colt. Blood made a dark

34

brown blotch in the sand. A few feet beyond the dead man's Stetson lay where it had fallen.

Cole dismounted, ground-reining the nervous bay, and bent over the body. He had a premonition who the man was even before he lifted the still face from the sand.

The buzzards had ripped at the gray's hindquarters, but left the man alone, except for a beak-slash below the right shoulder. Cole's throat tightened as he turned the man's face toward him.

He remained on his heels, looking down at his brother Bill. He was not a pretty sight.

Cole made himself a cigarette. It had been a long time since he had last seen Bill—his younger brother had been twelve when he left—and the shock of his death was remote. Cole had seen too many men die to have it affect him now. He blew out smoke and turned, his glance picking up tracks in the sand, reading with a trained eye the story of Bill's death.

His killer had come down the trail from the north and met Bill here in the arroyo as his brother was returning home. Cole reached out and picked up Bill's Colt, pulling it loose from clenched fingers. He blew sand out of the muzzle and swung the cylinder out. There was a bullet fired in it.

He looked down again on Bill's waxlike features, seeing here the boy he had taught to ride back on the old Cross B. He and Bill had been the youngest of the Barrett boys and they had taken a lot from their older brothers. Looking down at this man he remembered only as a boy, he wondered how it had been with him—how he had fared through the rough years of the Civil War.

These thoughts went through him, saddening him more than the first shock of seeing his brother lying here had done. After eight years a lot of the old bitterness had been swept away—he had seen too much senseless killing during the war years—and he had headed for Shadow Valley with the growing anticipation of seeing Bill and Jay and Barney again. And Martha, too. She should be a woman, now—married perhaps.

The sun was warm in his face when he straightened. He thrust Bill's weapon under his waistband and pulled the body free of the gray. His teeth set as he noticed Bill's left arm, almost severed just below the elbow.

His mount shied away as he approached it with the body. 'Easy, boy,' he soothed. 'Easy now.' He managed to get the stiff figure across the saddle and mounted. The bay tossed its head as he gathered up the reins.

'All right,' Cole muttered harshly. 'Let's go home.'

*   *   *

Martha Barrett tugged impatiently at her

36

yellow kid gloves as she walked across the yard to the ranchhand holding a saddled pinto. On the steps of the adobe house a stooped, rawboned man with a long white mustache watched her. He tried to hide the worry in his keen blue eyes.

The girl took the bridle from the wrangler's hand and mounted with the quick grace of one who had grown up in the saddle. Marcus Barrett came haltingly down the steps, leaning on his cane as she rode by.

'I'll kill him, Martha,' he exploded harshly, 'if you find him drunk in Spanish Rose's place again!'

Martha looked at him a little coldly, pityingly. She was a long-legged, dark-haired girl with her father's strong, bony features, his thin-lipped mouth, his sharp intolerance of any weakness. Her eyes were brown. In her mother they had been gentle and kind—in her they were dark and hard and unyielding.

There was a hardness in this woman that was like gray rock—the layer-on-layer hardness of a girl reared in a house dominated by its men. More than anything else in her childhood Martha had wanted their love and understanding—now, as a woman, she had only a barely hidden contempt for the lot of them.

'I'll get him home,' she answered, 'if I have to horse-whip him all the way!'

Marcus nodded. Until a skittish mount had

37

thrown him, breaking his hip, he had been as erect and hard-riding at sixty as any of them. But the accident had left him crippled. And because his ego had been fed by his physical stamina, his misfortune had left him suddenly old. His hair and mustache, a mixture of gray and black before, had whitened almost overnight. Even his voice had changed, lost its booming certainty. Often now it was wheedling.

'Better take the Salt Bluff trail, Martha,' he advised petulantly. 'If Bill's on his way home he'll be coming that way—it's shorter.'

He turned away from his daughter's glance, leaning heavily on his cane.

Martha turned the pinto toward the wide gate in the adobe wall. She was halfway across the yard when a rider came into view on the trail, his horse kicking up dust in the morning heat.

She thought it was Bill at first. There was a certain familiarity in the carriage of the rider. Then she noticed the body across the saddle and saw that the tilt of the campaign hat was definitely not that of her younger brother. She wheeled the pinto around in sudden alarm.

'Dad!' she called, stopping her father's ascent of the stairs. 'Someone's coming up the Salt Bluff trail now!'

Cole saw her come riding out of the ranchyard and he drew the bay up on the side of the road to wait. He recognized his sister as she neared—she had filled out a little, he noticed, but otherwise she had changed little. She had been seventeen, he remembered, the afternoon he had had his bitter quarrel on the porch of the old Brazos ranchhouse. He had cut loose from the family that night, and only his mother had indicated she understood.

Martha had always been a moody girl—sometimes sullen, often unexplainably gay. He read the changes in her now, the stony hardness and the unveiled bitterness. She jerked the pinto aside, hurting its mouth, and her sharp glance jumped from Bill to Cole.

In that one glance she saw that Bill was dead, and the shock of that dulled her perception so that she did not immediately recognize the lean, sun-darkened man in the Union garb.

She spurred up close and laid a hand on Bill's head, her eyes suddenly soft and hurt. She raised them to Cole's impassive face, a sick question in them, and then recognition cut like a whip across her face.

'Cole!'

He nodded, seeking words that would bridge the gap of the years between them. But he sensed an unscalable wall here, an hostility that was at once a barrier and a warning. He thrust aside his own feelings and said quietly: 'Hello, Martha.'

She stared at him. At seventeen, he remembered, she had disliked dressing like a man. Now she seemed content in a faded blue chambray shirt and a pair of Levis. Her boots were scuffed and dusty and her Stetson was old and smudged. He noticed these things because he remembered Martha as having been finicky in her dress and her person—and more than anything else this indicated how much Martha had changed.

He noticed, too, that she was staring at him without expression, and her tone had a colorless quality, neither glad nor hostile. 'Where did you find Bill?'

'On the trail,' he replied. 'About three hours from here.'

She turned from him again, running her hand through Bill's hair. 'And Dad thought he had made a night of it,' she said bleakly. A sudden revulsion of feeling shook her. She spurred around so that she was alongside Cole, and her glance was caught by the meaning of Cole's yellow-striped pants. A small flame burst in her eyes.

'Traitor!' she spat. 'You dirty yellowleg!' She jerked at her quirt, a blind anger draining her face of blood.

Cole reached out and caught hold of her arm. Her strength was a thing of unreasoning hate, and she almost wrenched free of him.

'The war's over, Martha,' he said grimly. 'I've come home.'

He felt the strength go out of her arm. '*No!*' she whispered intensely. 'No—the war will never be over—for me!'

She jerked her wrist out of his grasp and dropped her arm. The look she gave him was uncompromising. 'I'm not glad to see you,' she said harshly. 'But Dad thinks he needs you.' She turned and gestured toward the adobe house. 'He's waiting for you—the poor fool!'

Cole's lips tightened at the contempt in her tone. He felt the lash of his own bitterness, but it was tempered by a sense of compassion. This was his sister, Martha, this stony, sterile woman who had come to meet him.

*   *   *

The new Cross B ranchhouse was a big, two-storied adobe building, built to Spanish architecture, and now faded and yellowed and a little run down. The man who had saddled Martha's horse stood in the doorway of the blacksmith shop, watching. Cole recognized him. Old Hank Sommers. He saw recognition in the bent figure, but the man made no other sign and Cole rode past him to the man rising from a wicker chair on the vine-entwined veranda.

Cole pulled up by the steps. Martha swung the pinto aside, watching, keeping a wall of reserve between them.

Marcus Barrett came to the head of the stairs. His big fist quivered on the head of his cane. He stood bent and silent, his lined face

41

dark with blood.

The sun was warm against Cole's back and the stillness seemed to hold some of his father's old strength. The years fell away and for a brief moment he was a boy again, riding into his father's yard on the Brazos. Then the illusion passed and with a shock he realized that this white-haired man who faced him was someone he did not know . . .

'Cole,' Marcus whispered. 'You've come back. You've come back, Cole.'

Cole nodded. 'I got your note.'

The older man trembled. 'Cole—it's good to see you. Come on in—come in.' He stopped and looked at the dead man across Cole's saddle. 'That's Bill, ain't it?' He did not seem surprised, nor did his youngest son's death apparently affect him. 'Bring him inside,' he added a little impatiently. 'Bring him in.'

Cole dismounted. Hank came slowly across the yard, dragging his left leg. He said: 'Glad to see you back, Cole. We need you.' He stepped up and helped Cole pull his brother's body from the saddle. He wet his lips as Bill's head rolled grotesquely. The blood that had gushed over the younger Barrett's gray shirt had dried and browned.

'I'll *give you* a hand with him,' he said, and his eyes softened and there was pity in them.

They went up the steps with their burden. Marcus hobbled ahead, pushing open the door. Martha sat saddle for a moment, as if hesitating. All of a sudden she whirled the pinto.

Cole looked back over his shoulder. She was riding at a gallop for the gate and he wondered at her sudden flight. She was headed somewhere fast, and with a very definite purpose.

Hank said: 'She and Bill were quite close. This must have hit her hard.'

They stepped inside a long beamed-ceiling living room furnished with heavy Spanish pieces. They crossed over worn Persian rugs to a hallway that split the house in two. They turned into Bill's room and placed the body on the counterpane.

Marcus Barrett looked down at his youngest son. 'Jay was killed at Shiloh,' he said. He turned and looked at Cole, seeing the Union uniform he wore for the first time.

Cole waited for the anger of the man, the uncompromising hardness that had turned him away from his father when he was a youngster. But it was no longer there. Something had smashed the strength from Marcus Barrett.

'They told me,' he was saying, shaking his head. 'It don't matter, Cole. It don't matter at all. The war's over.'

'No,' Cole said bleakly. 'It doesn't matter.' He was thinking back along the years, to the day he had gone into a St. Louis recruiting station and volunteered for the Union Army. That was the day the news of Fort Sumter had been blazoned across the front pages of the *Dispatch*.

He had no politics, only the prodding of an anger that still rode him, and he had joined the Union forces out of a reaction to his father and what his father had stood for. It had been a personal thing, his enlistment, and it had lasted throughout the war. Now the props of his long anger were knocked from under him and he had nothing for his father save pity and a feeling of regret.

He said slowly, measuring his words, 'You mentioned trouble, Dad. But I never expected to be bringing Bill in with me—like this.'

Marcus turned away from the bed, sinking wearily into a chair. 'They've got us between them,' he said heavily. 'The Gillis brothers and the Aragons. Crowding us—hoping I'll break an' clear out—'

'Where's Barney?'

'Up on the benches west of here. By Cougar Canyon Breaks. He's got what's left of our crew.'

Marcus suddenly got up and stamped out of the room, leaving Cole standing. Hank said quietly: 'It's a long story, Cole. An' a bitter one. Mebbe you better wait an' get it all in one sittin' later on.'

They left Bill's body on the bed, covered by a sheet, and went back to the living room. Through the windows two riders showed up, passing through the gate.

'That's Mike,' Hank said, surprised. 'An' Baldy. Wonder what they're doin' back here?'

Cole headed for the veranda, Hank keeping pace. Marcus was already in his wicker chair. He got to his feet as the riders came into the yard.

The two men swung their mounts together and came toward the small group on the stairs. They were fifteen feet away when Mike recognized Cole.

He jerked his bronc sidewise and slashed his right hand down to his Colt!

Cole's gun broke the stillness, pounding heavily across the intervening distance. Mike's weapon jerked out of his hand and dropped into the dust by his horse's feet. And then the stillness came back into the yard, hot and violent with frustrated rage . . .

CHAPTER FIVE

Mike's horse minced nervously, trampling the dust. Baldy, a long slat of a man with a small, sharp face, put his hands on his head, thereby plainly indicating he wanted out of this particular quarrel.

Marcus came to his feet, leaning heavily on his cane. 'Mike!' he demanded harshly. 'What the devil was the reason for that?'

The stocky youngster's face was set in a

rigid mold. 'Who is he?' he asked thickly, looking at Cole. 'What's *he* doin' here?'

'This is my son! Cole Barrett!'

Mike stiffened, surprise wiping the anger from his face. 'In that uniform?'

Marcus nodded. He looked old and infirm as he stood there, leaning on his cane. There was no fight left in him.

'It's my son Cole,' he repeated, trying to justify himself to this hard-faced puncher. 'He's come back to help—'

'I'm particular who I work for—an' with!' Mike cut in harshly. 'An' I don't work for no man wearin' that uniform.' He spat into the dust as a measure of his contempt, minced his horse around, swung low out of the saddle and scooped up his Colt. He didn't look at Cole again. He slid the gun into his holster, heeling it in with a rough gesture.

Cole's bullet had torn a gash along the back of his right hand. Blood made a bright band that trickled down his wrist. The youngster gave it no attention. He turned his horse's head around with a savage jerk.

Marcus lifted his voice. 'You got three weeks' pay coming!'

'Keep it!' Mike flung back. Then he was gone, a hard, erect figure passing through the gate.

Baldy broke the silence. 'Mike was always kinda proddy,' he drawled.

Some of Marcus' old anger flickered up in

him. He turned his gaze to this man, his voice grim. 'You staying?'

Baldy shrugged.

'You'll be taking yore orders from Cole. Any objections?'

Baldy looked sidewise at Cole. He had been a trapper before the war—and he had not taken sides in the recent quarrel. 'None,' he answered quietly.

Cole holstered his gun. 'Glad you feel that way, Baldy,' he said. He moved away from his father, pausing so that he faced Baldy. 'Hank tells me you were up on the benches with Barney?'

Baldy nodded. He looked at Marcus, directing his answer to the old cattleman. 'Barney's run into trouble again. Someone stampeded our gather night before last. The boys are roundin' up the strays now.'

Marcus swore without much feeling. 'Anyone hurt?'

'Pablo. Part of the herd stampeded through camp. We buried the Mex.'

Marcus' glance went to Cole, as if waiting for his son to take over. Finally he said: 'You look done in, Baldy. Wash up an' join us inside. Ah Ling's getting dinner ready.'

Baldy said: 'Shore could use some good grub.' He glanced up at Cole, meeting Cole's glance for the first time. There was a hard, challenging look in his eyes that vanished behind a forced blandness. He turned his

47

cayuse around and rode to the bunkhouse.

Cole watched him go. He was thinking that Barney was a fool if he had dispatched two badly needed men to break this news to his father. One would have served as well and perhaps come in sooner.

He watched Baldy swing out of saddle at the corral gate. There were some things he intended to ask the lanky puncher, he decided. One of them was where he had been when Mike had ridden up to El Toro. Had he and Mike left Barney together and then split, meeting later to ride into the Cross B? And why had Mike ridden to El Toro's? Even with his little knowledge of terrain Cole knew that El Toro's was far from any direct route to the Cross B. Evidently Mike had not gone to the Mexican inn on orders from his brother Barney. Then upon whose orders?

Standing there, watching Baldy turn his cayuse into the corral, Cole felt the slackness of his father's ranch. It confused and irritated him. He had come prepared for trouble. But he found he would have to fight alone. He would receive little help from his father. And he had a feeling he would get little help from his brother.

'Why?' he thought angrily. 'What has happened to us?'

Hank's low voice broke across his seething thoughts. 'Nice-lookin' bay yo're ridin', Cole. But he looks like he kin stand a rest. I'll take

48

his rig off an' turn him loose into the corral.'

Cole nodded. 'See you at dinner, Hank.'

*   *   *

Ah Ling remembered Cole. His round face broke into smiles as he came out of the kitchen, bringing food to the table. 'Mister Cole,' he greeted him, 'it is indeed nice to have you back with us.' Ah Ling had been raised by English missionaries before he crossed the Pacific to be smuggled into the United States. He took solemn pride in his precise English.

'Glad to be eating your grub again, Ling,' Cole said, smiling. 'I missed it in the Army.'

Ling bobbed his head up and down, greatly pleased. Marcus settled himself in his chair at the head of the long table. 'Baldy'll be in to eat with us, Ling,' he informed. 'Hank, too.'

Baldy came in through the kitchen. He had washed and shed his chaps. He had shaved recently, Cole noticed. Black pinpoints of beard were just beginning to show on his face, heavy around his mouth and chin and straggly on his leathery cheeks. A sparse growth of earth-colored hair had been combed across the bald top of his head.

'Hank told me about Bill,' he said, pulling out a chair. He shot a look at Cole. 'Looks like hell's gonna be a quiet place alongside these parts for the next few days.'

Cole frowned. 'Why?'

49

Baldy sat down. He looked at Marcus, as if expecting the older man would explain. But the cattleman was staring gloomily at his plate. Baldy settled back and said to Cole: 'There's a crazy Mex that goes loco every time the moon gets full. Nobody knows who the galoot is, but he shore raises Ned around here for three or four days a month.'

He dug into his pocket for his Bull Durham and was silent while he made himself a smoke. Cole was watching him, waiting, staring moodily over the valley, his thoughts going back to Sebastian.

'He killed Slim right here in the bunkhouse last month,' Baldy continued. 'Mike was with Slim. Rest of us were up with Barney. First thing Mike knew this hombre in chest armor was in the bunkhouse, swinging a sword—'

'A sword?'

Baldy nodded. 'He fancies the long cutter, but he shore kin handle a Colt if he gets into a tight spot. Rides around in Spanish armor an' a cloak an' kin move like a lobo on the kill. Owns a palomino any man in the valley, including old Pedro Aragon, would give his right arm for. Nobody knows who he is, or where he's from. Doesn't seem to bother any of the Mexes in the valley, though. There's a lot of talk—' Baldy shrugged, grinning a little sheepishly as if he suddenly felt he had talked too much. He began to concentrate on the food Wah Ling brought in.

Cole glanced at his father. The other man was staring moodily at the wall, apparently unmoved by Baldy's recital. It was fantastic. A crazy Mexican who terrorized the valley and killed when the moon got full. The man must have killed his brother Bill last night. Yet Baldy imparted the information almost casually, and his father made no comment.

Cole felt a little sick. The apathy in the room was like dry rot, and it revolted him. What's gone wrong? he thought bitterly. What's happened here?

Hank came in, limping. His leathery face, crisscrossed by innumerable age lines, was strangely soothing. There was no bitterness in it, only a kindly humor enlivened by his bright blue eyes under shaggy gray brows.

He sat down beside Cole as Ling came into the room. There was little conversation during dinner. Marcus ate little. Baldy ate silently, but with hunger, and pushed away as soon as he was through. 'Guess I'll saddle up a fresh mount an' get back to Barney,' he said to Cole. 'Barney's short-handed as anything. Lake an' Cardo quit yesterday, right after the stampede. An' now with Mike gone—'

Marcus cut in sharply: 'Lake an' Cardo quit, you say?'

Baldy nodded. 'They had an argyment with Barney.'

Marcus looked at Cole. The younger man felt the responsibility that was being placed on

51

his shoulders with that look. He had come home, and now he knew he wouldn't have time to look around, to get the feel of trouble.

'How many men left with Barney?' he asked.

'Three. Four, countin' myself.'

Cole remembered the apparent friendliness of Mike with the Saber men. 'I ran into Mike up at a Mexican place called El Toro,' he said. 'He was there with a couple of Saber riders.' He grinned wryly. 'One of 'em called himself Cash Gillis, offered me a riding job.'

His hard glance pinned Baldy. 'What was Mike doing up at El Toro's? And where were you?'

Baldy hunched forward in his chair. His eyes moved to Marcus, who had straightened, and came back to Cole's unfriendly regard.

'Mike an' I left the Breaks together,' he admitted. 'I stopped by the Long Creek linehouse to see if there were any supplies we could use. Mike headed for El Toro's on an errand for Barney.' He hesitated, then grinned coolly. 'If you gotta know, Barney wanted a bottle of whiskey bad. Mike said he'd bring him back one. El Toro's was nearer than San Ramos—'

Cole looked at his father then, a sharp question in his glance. But the older man averted his gaze. So that's how it is, Cole thought dismally. We're licked before we even start!

Baldy said blandly: 'I met Mike again this mornin' an' we rode in together. I didn't know he had had trouble with you at El Toro's.'

Cole shrugged.

Baldy pushed away from the table. 'If it's all the same, I'll get back to Barney.' He looked directly at Cole. 'Barney said he needed grub an' more men. Both in a hurry!'

Cole said: 'Ling'll let you have what he can spare out of the chuck shack. I'll go into town for more later. About extra hands, tell Barney I'll see what I can do.'

Baldy butted his cigarette out in his plate. 'I'll tell him,' he nodded. He turned and walked out.

Hank said: 'Wait a minnit, Baldy. I'll ride up with you.' He turned to Cole. 'I'm not much good in the saddle, but I kin cook. I kin take Pablo's place up there.' He smiled briefly. 'I'll tell Barney yo're back.'

He followed Baldy, and Cole looked at his father. There were a lot of things he wanted to say, but he was like a stranger here—a stranger suddenly given the responsibility of running a ranch he knew little about. He felt like reaching over and shaking the gray, thin-cheeked man and saying: 'Wake up, Dad! What's happened?'

But the words wouldn't come and only his irritation stirred and made his voice sharp. 'Dad, what's left of the old outfit we had?'

Marcus explained, without interest, 'The

war took most of them. A few drifted back an' stuck with us when we came here. Hank, Ah Ling, Potley, Long Bob an' Slim Evans. Potley, Long Bob an' a new hand named Beecher are with Barney. Slim was killed last month, like Baldy said. Mike an' Baldy an' the two punchers who just quit Barney were picked up in town. Martha hired them.' He caught the look in Cole's eye and flushed ashamedly. 'Hang it all, Cole, I can't get around any more. An' Barney's a hermit. He won't leave the Breaks. Bill? I never could depend on him.'

Cole said quietly: 'Just what are we up against?'

Marcus rubbed his stubbled chin. 'I kinda forget you just got here, son. Seems like you've always been around somehow. Quiet fella, not so big an' loud-talking as yore brothers. Took more after Margaret . . .' His voice petered off into sad reflection, and Cole had difficulty remembering that this beaten man was the big, domineering person he had rebelled against.

'It was Barney's idea that we came here,' Marcus went on. 'We decided to move right after Barney came home. We had nothing left except a thousand head of beef, mostly four and five year olds. An' the old place didn't seem the same without you an' Jay. Barney came back restless. Moody, too. An' Martha—' He shrugged, and a slight frown crinkled his thinning brows. 'Well, you've seen Martha.' He continued. 'We sold out, except for the stock,

54

an' headed west looking for a new place to settle. Barney rode on ahead. He met young Perez de Gama in Tucson. Black sheep son of the de Gamas, I gathered. He had just inherited this place in Shadow Valley, an' didn't know what to do with it. He didn't want to come back, an' Barney talked me into buying him out.'

Cole listened. His father was talking without enthusiasm, like a man patiently getting something off his chest.

'This place was given to the original de Gamas on a land grant. Long before this valley became Texas territory the de Gamas and the Aragons ran it between them. There was one other haciendado in the valley, an eccentric grandee who built a big place on one of the buttes flanking the old trail that came in through the Conquistadores. The Pueblos used to raid out of the hills, an' this Spaniard built his home up on the butte for protection. They say there was only one way up, a narrow trail easily guarded. Somehow, the Pueblos surprised the guard one night and got up. They massacred the old Don's entire family. The grandee was down in San Ramos that afternoon and escaped. When he rode back an' saw what had happened he went crazy. He bought a keg of giant powder, hauled it up the trail an' blew himself an' the trail to smithereens. No one's been up there since.'

Marcus hesitated a moment, then went on.

55

'Our real trouble's with the Gillis brothers an' Pedro Aragon. The Gillis boys came into the valley about four months behind us. They run the Saber outfit. They came in on a shoestring an' settled across the only good trail out of the valley, the trail through the Pinnacles. For a shoestring outfit they've been growin' mighty fast.

'The Aragons are southwest of us. Their range runs down to the Rio Grande. Pedro Aragon hated de Gama an' passed on that hatred to us. He's got a son an' a daughter. Julio's a weaklin'. But if you stay in the valley a while you'll meet Juanita Aragon—she's a spitfire. Sometimes I think she an' their foreman, a hardcase named Manuel, really run the Aragon spread.

'Pedro Aragon's been losin' cows. Naturally he's suspicious of us an' Saber. We're nearest. Saber's way over on the other side of us an' they'd have to run any of Aragon's beeves across our range. You see how the old Dons thinkin'?'

Cole nodded. 'We're caught in the middle. Saber's raidin' us an' the Aragons, an' gettin' away with it.'

'That's the way it is, son. We were broke when we got here. Then we began hearin' about the markets openin' up in Kansas an' the Indian Territory. We had more than a thousand head an' de Gama didn't even know how many of his father's cattle were left. We started roundin' up everythin' on our range an' slappin' our iron on them. We got close to a thousand more head together an' I put a trail crew with it, under Barney. I promised every man a bonus if they got the herd to market—'

He laughed shrilly. 'That's when we ran into our first trouble. The Gillis boys have strung barbed wire across the trail at Horseshoe Pass an' put up a "No Trespassing" sign. They had men patrolling it. We had to trail through the Horseshoe to get out of the valley, an' Cash Gillis knew it.

'I rode out an' had a talk with Gillis. He didn't back down. Wanted two dollars a head for everything that passed through Horseshoe Pass, plus one cow out of every twenty. I told him to go to blazes. He laughed in my face. I went back an' told Barney an' the boys how it was. We made a try for it. We lost two men an' most of the cattle we had sweated to get together. After that the new men quit. Then the cayuse I was ridin' went skittish on me at the wrong time, pilin' me on some rocks. I broke my hip . . .'

Cole nodded, beginning to see how it was. A long string of tough luck can break the spirit of a man. But there was more to it than this, he thought grimly. The Barretts weren't the kind to break under luck, good or bad. There was a dry rot here that could be traced to the war. It had affected almost everyone he knew, those who had gone into it and those who had stayed behind.

Even so, he thought wearily, a man just can't let himself go to pieces. He's got to fight, keep on fighting. Because when he quits, he's through—and nothing has meaning any more.

He got up and looked out of the window, surprised to see that the afternoon had worn on. The sun shed a mellow light on the dust in the yard. He felt something stir inside him, a deep longing, and it came to him then that this was what he had been looking for since Appomattox—an end to his restless moving and a chance to dig in and take root.

Marcus was looking at him, a strange eagerness in his lined face. 'You'll take over, Cole?' he asked. 'I can't get around. An' Barney won't listen. He stays away from the ranch an' drinks—'

'I'll see what I can do,' Cole interrupted quickly. He remembered Bill then, and what had to be done. Best get it over with while Baldy and Hank were still here.

'Where did Bill go yesterday?'

Marcus' eyes softened, as if the fact of his youngest son's death were just beginning to get through his numbed emotions. 'Sent him down to San Ramos,' he said in a dry whisper. 'He was to hire riders. An' I thought he had passed the night with one of the girls at Spanish Rose's place.'

Cole saw the gray misery in his father's eyes then and he said softly: 'We best bury him

58

while Hank and Baldy are still here.'

*   *   *

They dug a grave for the youngest Barrett beside that of his mother in the old de Gama cemetery, a small, walled-in plot on a knoll overlooking the creek. Cole had driven the buckboard, with his father silent on the seat beside him and the long rough coffin quickly put together by Hank riding on the wagon bed behind them. Hank remembered a few lines from Scripture and quoted them haltingly over the grave, while Baldy stood by, no expression on his long face. When it was over Hank said goodbye and rode off with the tall rider, leaving Cole and Marcus to return to the ranch alone.

Cole was thinking of Martha as he turned in that night. He was still awake, restless and vaguely irritable, when he heard someone ride into the yard. He got up and looked out the window.

Martha was turning her cayuse loose in the big corral. The bright half-moon was on her. She moved like a man, briskly and with purpose, and as she turned and came across the yard toward the house he saw her face. The hardness was gone from it. It was soft and feminine and her eyes had a soft shine to them.

59

CHAPTER SIX

Martha did not join them for breakfast. Cole ate with his father, who stared blankly over his food. Cole could see the disintegration in him. Marcus had not shaved in days and the gray-streaked beard intensified the gauntness of his cheeks.

Cole pushed back and lighted a cigarette. He wanted to get away from here, to get outside where he could think.

'Everything's gone to blazes since the war,' Marcus said abruptly. He was scowling at Cole. 'Bill grew up wild. I couldn't handle him any more. Neither could Barney. Only Martha had a way with him. And she—' Marcus sucked in his lips. His eyes had a suddenly bewildered look. 'She's changed too, Cole. She used to be pretty an' liked to laugh. She had a temper, remember. But she's changed. She's cold an' hard an' she doesn't care for any of us. It's been like that since her husband was killed.'

'Husband?' Cole turned around. 'Looks like there's some family history I need catching up on.'

'She married Johnny Vickers a year after you left. I thought I told you—' Marcus wagged his head silently. 'They were married a month. Then Vickers joined the Texas Volunteers. He was killed with Jay at Chicka-

60

maugua.'

Cole thought: So that's it—that's why my sister hates me! And a somber mood darkened his spirits.

'Barney came back in one piece,' his father added stonily. 'But he's not the old Barney. Drinks too much now. Wants to be by himself.' He looked at Cole. 'You haven't changed, Cole,' he observed, and there was a wistfulness in his voice that tightened Cole's throat. 'You never talked loud. But yo're tough inside. Tougher than the rest of us. You won't break. You'll fight.' He repeated the phrase, making it a sharp question. 'You'll fight?'

Cole nodded. 'Sure—we'll fight!' He made it 'we' and knew that he had pleased the broken man across the table. He got up then and left the room. The atmosphere was unhealthy and he wanted to get outside.

He stood a moment in the bright morning sunlight, looking about him. The bunkhouse door was open and sagging on a broken hinge. Somehow it brought together the mood of the Cross B—a ranch deserted and falling to pieces. Flower beds planned and set up around the house by the de Gamas had evidently gone unattended since the death of his mother. The north wall of the patio in the rear needed repair. Harness needed mending. Tools were rusting in the blacksmith shop.

'Goin' to blazes!' his father had said.

Cole roped a roan stallion from the bunch

61

in the corral and saddled him. He felt someone watching him from the house as he worked, and when he drew the cinches tight and swung lightly up into the saddle he turned and glanced toward the building.

Martha was at her bedroom window. She didn't draw back as he looked, nor did she make any sign of recognition. The stony look she had worn when they had first met confronted him now, defying his attempts at reconciliation.

He swung the roan and cantered out of the yard, feeling a gray loneliness envelop him. Where was the fight in the Cross B? Cattle were being rustled, they were bottled up in the valley, and Bill had evidently been killed by some locoed killer in armor. And no one was doing anything about it.

He tilted his hat over his eyes and leaned into the sun. Already the heat was shimmering in the hollows. He rode at a lope, not heading in any particular direction, just glad to get away from the dull apathy that seemed to hang over the ranch buildings. When he topped a small rise, he pulled up and turned his lean body in the saddle.

The Cross B, with its outbuildings, was laid out before him, like square, dun-colored blocks surrounded by an adobe wall. Cottonwoods made an avenue from the wider road to the adobe gate, cottonwoods evidently planted at an earlier time by the de Gamas. A half-mile south of the buildings a water tank caught the overflow from the springs and provided water and shade for the Cross B cattle nearer home. Irrigation ditches engineered by the early Zunis and later converted by the de Gamas used to channel the overflow from the springs to tilled land behind the hacienda. The sides of the ditches, in many places, had fallen in now, and weeds had sprung up, partially obliterating old channels.

Looking from this vantage point, Cole clearly saw the extent of the decay. The de Gamas had had pride in their land, but the Barretts didn't care.

He let his roan pick its own pace now, and idle curiosity led him back along the Salt Bluff trail. When he got to the dry creek where he had found his brother's body, he stopped.

The buzzards and the coyotes had been back at the cayuse. There was little left except bones. Of the scavenger he had shot he saw only a few scattered feathers.

He left the trail and swung south. His father had expected him to ride up to see Barney. But Cole decided he'd see his brother later. He cut across the rolling rangeland that became more fertile as he approached Aragon country. The old grandee's range was bounded by Salt Creek on the west, a dry watercourse angling across the long valley.

He heard the slam of a carbine as he

63

rounded a small hillock. Cole eased forward in his saddle, his eyes suddenly watchful.

The shots seemed to punch through the hot stillness somewhere ahead, hidden among the breaks of the creek. They were methodical strokes of sound, as though someone were shooting unhurriedly at a target.

The roan minced nervously under Cole, its sides heaving. Gun-shy, Cole surmised. He reined in and stroked the dusty mane. 'Easy, boy.'

The stallion quit mincing and fighting the bit, but it kept trembling as it walked. Cole eased his weight back in the saddle, loosened his holster gun, and rode toward the rifle shots.

He went down a slope that was scarred by small arroyos carrying the runoff into Salt Creek. Prickly pear and chaparral lined the banks. Cole eased his way through thorny bush, following an old cattle trace to the edge of Salt Creek. Other cattle paths converged here and a runway had been worn down to the creek bed by steers seeking the small water pools under the shaded cut-banks.

Cole dismounted. He looped his reins over a thorn limb and eased ahead, his Colt sliding into his fist. The creek bed was about fifty yards wide and the sun filtered through the tall mesquite trees lining the banks. The body of a cow lay plainly visible on the hot sand just below him. There was another carcass further on, and around a shallow pool of stagnant, slimy water were several others. Flies buzzed busily over the dead cattle.

Cole's glance came back to the steer almost directly below him. The Cross B brand was plainly visible on the still flank. The body was still warm, and blood glistened from the bullet hole under its ear. Cole went down the runway and walked to the animal. A horse snorted loudly in the deep stillness. Cole wheeled and faced the sound.

Three men rode into view past the stagnant pool and drew up sharply at sight of the lone man standing over the carcass. They were Mexican vaqueros, evidently Aragon men. But it was the hombre in the middle who held Cole's attention. He was a well built fellow about Cole's height and weight and he rode relaxed and easy. But there was a quality about him that reminded Cole of a mountain cat, all easy grace and deadly power. He was wearing a dark green charro jacket, not fancy, and his dark face was shaded from the hot sun by a huge Mexican sombrero. He lounged indolently in the saddle, a carbine held lightly across the pommel. A pearl-handled Colt snuggled in a tooled-leather holster.

For just a moment his eyes widened. The man on his left sucked in his breath and ejaculated: 'Calico!'

The thought went through Cole then that this was the second time he had been taken for

65

a man named Calico. And judging from the reactions he had encountered, this Calico was a man to be reckoned with.

He said sharply: 'Look again, gents. And you in the middle, don't make any fancy moves with that carbine.'

The man addressed relaxed, a thin smile warping the side of his hard mouth. He was a handsome man in a careless, offhand way that usually went well with women. But his diffidence now was a shield and Cole knew it.

'*Por dios*, Melio,' he said to the rider on his left. 'He is not Calico. He is *un estranjero*, no?' He looked at Cole, his eyes lidded. 'You work for the Cross B, perhaps.'

'Perhaps.'

'An' what you see,' the Mexican foreman continued, 'does not please you?'

'A man usually has a reason for killing another man's cattle,' Cole countered grimly. 'I'm waiting to hear yours.'

The other chuckled. 'You are new here,' he sneered, 'or you would know that this is Aragon land. From here,' he tilted his head slightly to the south and west, 'to the Rio. An' the Aragons intend to keep their land!'

'By killing cows?' Cole cut in sardonically.

'An' men if need be,' the other added coolly. 'Especially those who ride for the gringo, Marcus Barrett.'

'What have you got against the Barretts?'

The Mex spat insolently. 'Listen close, *mi*

66

amigo. You will find it much healthier if you do not work for the Cross B. It is good advice I am giving you, *señor.*'

'And who is giving me this advice?'

'Manuel Ortega,' the other said, and eyes flashed with sudden arrogance. 'And now, when you return, you can tell Marcus Barrett that every cow bearing his brand that crosses Salt Creek will be shot and left for the buzzards. And that, *señor,* will go for every one of his riders as well.'

A smile crinkled Cole's lips. 'Seven cows,' he said, as if he had not heard the other's boast. He recounted the carcasses with the muzzle of his Colt. 'I'll be calling at the Aragon hacienda for the price of those steers, Manuel. And for every other Cross B cow you or your men kill, the price will double.'

Manuel sneered. 'That's big talk, *amigo*— for a cowhand—'

'Not just a cowhand,' Cole interrupted coldly. 'I'm Cole Barrett!'

Manuel's feigned indolence vanished. He stared with sudden alertness, a slow smile breaking the iron slit of his lips. 'I heard there was another Barrett,' he said finally. 'But you do not look like the others.'

'My looks suit me,' Cole snapped. 'Now get moving, and keep going. And remember, Manuel—for every cow you kill from now on in old Pedro will pay double!'

He waited while the Aragon men wheeled

around and rode back the way they had come. Once out of sight, he turned and ran back to his roan and led it out of the thick brush. He mounted and skirted the high ground, and when he finally turned for a look the three men he had encountered in the creek bottom were vague small figures heading south . . .

CHAPTER SEVEN

San Ramos lay between two small hills. An Aztec village, it had been old when Cortez cantered up the trail from Mexico City. The later Spaniards, led by Father Domingas, built the mission of San Ramos with the help of the pacified Zunis, and added several two-story adobe structures around the drowsy plaza. The presidio they built on the other hill, so that the flag of Spain faced the cross on the mission, twin symbols of Spanish power.

The mission had weathered the changing years, but the Spanish fort had fallen into disrepair, its encircling adobe wall crumbling in the hot sun.

It was past noon when Cole reached town. He jogged the roan up the dusty main street, past the squalor of the Mexican hovels where dirty-faced children played in the dust, red chile hung like banners from the eaves and goats wandered restlessly around their holding

68

stakes, baaing insolently at every passerby.

The newer section of San Ramos, inhabited recently by hardcases from east of the Pecos, held several false-fronted pine slab structures that bore American titles. DAVE's HAY & FEED. KELLY'S LUNCHROOM. CHARLES BRISTER, ATTORNEY AT LAW. THE LONE STAR SALOON.

Cole watered the roan at the water trough in the middle of the drowsy plaza, then turned and rode to the Lone Star's hitchrail. A lanky man with a star on his calfskin vest glanced at Cole with sharp-eyed scrutiny. He had a hard, leathery face of indeterminate age, a short brown thick mustache and a pair of guns set in high, tooled-leather holsters. He was reclining lazily in a chair in the shade cast by the Lone Star's slanting wooden awning, and he was in a position thereby to observe every rider who entered San Ramos by the upvalley trail.

Cole went past him and pushed through the slatted doors. He felt the interior coolness against his heated face and the raw smell of liquor and tobacco smoke was sharp after the dryness of the trail. There was a bar of polished wood along the east wall and tables along the other. A poker game was going on with the five men sitting in it displaying desultory interest. A tattered oldster with dirty gray hair growing shaggily down his dirty neck was nursing a beer at the end of the bar. The bartender looked bored.

Cole walked to the bar and turned his attention to the big man dozing at the end of the counter. The man pushed himself off his elbows and came toward Cole, yawning sleepily, showing two gold-capped uppers. He was in shirtsleeves, rolled to his elbows. His hairy forearm was as thick as Cole's thigh. He had sleepy eyes the color of pale beer, and there was a guarded tightness around his wide mouth.

'What's yores?' he asked sleepily.

'Whiskey.'

Bull Harness flipped a glass onto the bar and set a bottle up in front of Cole. 'Help yoreself, stranger.'

Cole poured and Harness leaned on the bar. 'Just get yore discharge?' he made talk. There was no particular partisanship in Bull's question. Bull had taken no sides in the recent war between the States, being politically on the fence and legally outside the law. He had left Louisville ten years ago, having killed a man over a girl, and drifting west, had finally found San Ramos to his liking.

Cole shrugged. He wanted information, but he knew Harness' type, and he decided to act close-mouthed.

Harness pulled at his lower lip, frowning slightly. 'Driftin' through to the border?'

Cole finished his drink. 'Mebbeso.' He poured himself another shot and left it to make himself a smoke.

70

A rider drew up before the saloon rail and hailed the man on the porch. A moment later his bulk loomed up against the batwings. He was a blond man, taller than Cole and heavier—handsome in a cold, ruthless way. He walked with a quick, restless stride, his eyes alert and gun-muzzle blue. He came up to he bar, sizing Cole and reserving judgment, pushing it back into some niche in his mind.

Harness said: 'Howdy, Tom,' and reached under the bar for a special brand of rye whiskey.

The other poured, said: 'Where's the kid?'

Harness nodded toward a rear door. The blond man tossed down his drink, set the glass back on the bar and walked to the rear door.

Cole observed idly: 'I'm lookin' for work. Know who's hirin'?'

Harness' eyes widened a little. He tilted his head and glanced at the gun in Cole's low-slung holster, and a veiled caution came into his voice.

'You passed right by the O Slash Seven if you came into the valley by way of Horseshoe Canyon.'

Cole shook his head. 'Followed an old Spanish trail through the Conquistadores. Some fool up at Bent's Ford said it was the shortest way to the border an' I happened to be in a hurry.' He saw Harness' eyes light up understandingly, and he threw in casually: 'Stopped for a couple of drinks at a place

71

called El Toro's on the road. Heard some queer stories along with the whiskey. Seems there's a Mexican ghost who gets proddy every time the moon fills up an' goes prowlin' around with a sword—'

Harness sneered. 'Carlos is as cracked as that fire-eatin' nephew of his. I ben hearin' the same stories, stranger. I never seen the hombre, though the Mexs around here swear they have. They cross themselves every night the moon is full—an' it makes 'em go to church regular, anyway.' The big barman laughed, a booming sound that shook his big belly. 'I'd like to see thet Mex ghost show up here just once. Ain't never heard of no armor that could stop a slug from a .45.

He turned and nodded toward the rear door. 'That was Tom Gillis who just came in, stranger. He an' his brother, Cash, run the O Slash Seven. I think they're hirin', if yo're willin' to slap a saddle on trouble.'

'Been ridin' it all my life,' Cole answered mildly. 'What kind of trouble?'

Harness' eyes narrowed. 'Range trouble.'

Cole looked disinterested. He took a pull at his drink and toyed with the glass. 'The O Slash Seven the only outfit in the valley?'

'There's two others,' Harness admitted. 'The Cross B an' a Mex outfit, the Triple A. There's a couple of smaller ranches along the river, but they're too far an' they don't count anyway.' He studied Cole surreptitiously. 'The

72

Cross B's the biggest American outfit, but I wouldn't work for 'em if I was you.'

'No?'

Harness grunted. 'It's fallin' to pieces. They might hire you, though—they're shorthanded. Pay's mostly on promise. The Triple A's southwest of here. Pedro Aragon's got the best kept spread in the valley. He's been here a long time on a land grant. Uppity customer for a Mex on Texas land. Claims to be havin' trouble with rustlers an' has orders out to shoot anyone trespassin'.'

Cole fingered his drink. 'Feller playin' his cards right oughta get in on somethin' good, eh?' he said significantly. Then he glanced toward the door. 'Who's the craggy badgetoter on your porch?'

Harness chuckled. 'Buck Gaines? No need to step easy on his account, stranger. Buck's got a fast hand with a Colt, so we 'lected him town marshal. He keeps order in San Ramos. Keeps the Mexs in line.'

Cole grinned. 'Nice arrangement,' he said admiringly. He turned on his elbow and went suddenly alert as the rear door opened and two men came out.

One was Tom Gillis. The other, carrying his right arm in a sling, was the youngster he had twice had trouble with—the man named Mike. They were heading for the front door when the youngster's casual glance picked on Cole. Barrett saw surprise twitch through him. Mike

73

stopped dead, his voice suddenly loud and clear in the drowsy room.

'Wait a minnit, Tom!'

Tom turned impatiently. Mike kept his eyes on Cole. 'That's him,' he said bleakly. 'That's Cole Barrett!'

CHAPTER EIGHT

Tom Gillis was a good judge of men. He was a hard man himself, with a dangerous temper only lightly held in check by a humorous streak which often made him unpredictable. One never knew when Tom Gillis would explode or laugh. He was the younger of the Gillis brothers, a man of about twenty-seven, and he was big enough to usually get what he wanted.

He looked at Cole now, taking in the lean, dusty figure in cavalryman's pants, measuring him in one hurried glance. Then he smiled, but his eyes had a flat, unfriendly light.

'Cole Barrett,' he said, crinkling an eyebrow. 'Didn't know the old man had another son.'

Harness had gone tense behind the bar, the sleepiness vanished. The poker players had turned watchful, expectant faces toward Cole. Mike was standing like a big dog with his fur up.

Tom Gillis walked to the bar. 'You runnin'

things at the Cross B now?'

'Sort of.'

'Too bad,' Tom murmured. 'I hear it's in bad shape.' He nodded at Harness, who reached under the bar again for Gillis' special brand of whiskey. He poured his shot and slid the bottle to Cole, and his smile was now frank and easy. 'I found out early that Bull carries only two kinds of likker,' he said. 'That which he serves his customers an' the brand he keeps for himself. I like his brand best. Try it.'

Cole thought: So this is Tom Gillis? and reserved further judgment. He said aloud: 'It can't be worse than I just had,' and poured himself a drink.

Mike came up now, bristling, his eyes puzzled. 'That's a Barrett!' he said harshly, wonderingly. 'What are you gonna do about him, Tom?'

Tom answered mildly: 'Why, I'm goin' to have a drink with him, Mike.' He turned to Cole, a thoughtful glint in his eyes. 'You the Lieutenant Barrett in charge of the company that held out at Horseshoe Ridge?'

Cole shrugged. 'The Rossville road?'

'I was on the other side,' Gillis said. '15th Texas Regiment. We thought we were headed straight for Chattanooga that time—' He stopped, his smile thinning. 'Wonder why a Texan fought under Sheridan?'

'It's a long story,' Cole said bleakly. 'I don't think you'd find it interesting.'

'Mebbe not,' the other murmured. He took his drink, savoring it. 'You figgerin' to run cattle up to Abilene?'

'Soon as we can throw a herd together,' Cole answered coldly.

'I hear prices are goin' up all the time,' Gillis said. 'Started at seven dollars a head—now I hear they're up to fifteen. Not bad when you consider that a year or two ago you couldn't give a cow away.'

'Not bad at all,' Cole agreed.

'Reckon you won't mind payin' two dollars a head to drive up the Pinnacle trail, then?' Gillis asked.

Cole pushed his drink aside. 'We're paying no one,' he said levelly. 'Least of all a bunch of thieves.'

Gillis smiled. 'Yo're talkin' big for a man with a broken down outfit.'

'Big enough to make it stick!' Cole snapped. 'We're coming through the Pinnacles the next time, Gillis, if we have to blast our way through!'

Mike pushed himself forward. 'Damn it, Tom—I told yuh—'

Cole swung on him, his voice grating. 'You shut up!'

Mike's face whitened. He started for Cole, but Tom stopped him. He kept his eyes on Cole. 'We'll be waitin' for you—when you come up the trail,' he said. He turned and nodded at Harness and walked out, pushing a

76

stiff-legged Mike ahead of him.

Cole watched them go. Behind him he heard Bull Harness let out a long breath.

CHAPTER NINE

It was very quiet in the saloon after that. Cole tossed money on the counter and turned on his heel. He crossed to the door and paused on the shaded porch, watching Mike and Tom Gillis canter out of town.

A spring wagon was raising dust on the valley trail. Cole saw Tom rein in, lift his hat, and turn to watch the wagon roll past. It came on into town and Cole saw that it was Martha in the seat.

She drove past him without looking at him and pulled up before Jake's General Store. Cole walked across the street and intercepted her as she tied the mare to the rail and turned to the steps. She started to walk past him, her mouth pinching in coldly, but he held out a hand and stopped her.

'I heard about Johnny Vickers, Martha,' he said. 'I'm sorry.'

She looked up at him. 'Sorry for what?'

He kept his temper. 'A lot of good men were killed in the war,' he said quietly. 'Good men on both sides. I happened to be on the other side from Johnny Vickers. But the war's over

77

now. It would be a good thing if we remembered that—the war's over.'

Her lips curled. 'Maybe it is, for you. It's over for Jay and Johnny. But it'll never be over for me. I didn't want you back here. I didn't ever want to see you again. As far as I'm concerned you're not my brother. Now get out of my way!'

He let her go and she stepped past him and went into Jake's store. He waited on the shaded walk, letting his dark and dismal mood simmer down.

He had come to San Ramos to get the feel of things and perhaps to hire men for the roundup Barney was conducting. But he knew he'd get no help in town. He felt the squeeze that was being put on the Cross B, grinding it between the Gillis outfit on the north and the Aragon spread to the south. It seemed like a hopeless fight, and for a moment he felt like chucking it all and heading back north. Then his father's broken, yet strangely eager voice came back to him and he knew he could not let him down.

He turned on his heel and started back for the Lone Star rail. The girl in the doorway said: 'It was a long war, soldier. But I didn't think you'd forget that easily.'

He stopped and looked at her, frowning a little. She had evidently just come down from the long flight of steps leading to Attorney Brister's office and had stopped in the

78

doorway to adjust her hat. She was a tall, long-legged girl with a cool, pleasant face, and her eyes were gray and friendly. It was this friendliness that caught him.

'Your memory needs improvement,' she smiled. 'It was Lieutenant Barrett when we first met.'

He probed back into his memory until the connection was made. 'Ann Brister!' he recalled.

'You ignored me somewhat embarrassingly,' she said, 'the day Captain Deval of the fierce mustachios introduced us at the officers' ball at Fort Garrett. But I forgive you.'

He laughed. 'I was new at being a second lieutenant,' he remembered, 'and I was scared stiff. But,' he glanced up the street, 'San Ramos is not the place I'd have thought to see Charley Brister's daughter again.'

A shadow passed swiftly across her face and then a twinkle came into her eyes. 'Fortune is a rather fickle mistress, Lieutenant. It smiles and frowns where it may. And San Ramos does have a charm of its own, shall we say?'

He nodded, smiling, and she added: 'I was about to step out to lunch, and you look rather hungry to me.'

'Now that you've brought it to my mind,' he said gallantly, 'I am. You name the place; I'm new in town.'

She fell in beside him and they headed down the street. 'There's Pablo's place, the

79

Golden Ass.' Her eyes twinkled. 'You're like a breath from the north. And I willingly admit that sight of your uniform is refreshing. Are you here on duty?'

He shook his head. 'I've resigned my commission. My father moved into the valley right after the war and I've come home to help out. He owns the Cross B.'

She stopped and looked up at him, a faint shadow on her face. 'The Cross B. You mean you're one of *those* Barretts?'

He said: 'Yes, I'm one of those Barretts.' His voice was hard and his temper conveyed itself to her, for she added quickly: 'I'm sorry I said it that way. But you were an officer in the Union Army, and I thought—' She hesitated, and her confusion brought color into her cheeks.

He said quietly: 'You mean you don't understand why a Texan should have been wearing this uniform?'

'That's it.' Her voice was without judgment.

He took her arm, his temper subsiding. 'It's a longer story than you may like to hear. But if you'll listen I'll tell you why in Pablo's . . .'

*   *   *

Back at the Lone Star, Buck Gaines, an interested observer, slowly got to his feet and went into the saloon. Harness was behind the bar, still scowling thoughtfully.

'Craggy hombre, thet dark fella who jest left,' the marshal observed, sliding a Mexican cheroot between his stained teeth. 'Friendly with the Brister gal, too.'

Harness swore. 'That was Cole Barrett, old Marcus' boy. I thought he was a renegade soldier driftin' through here an' I let him pump me.'

Gaines turned this bit of information over in his mind. 'Does Tom know?'

'He does now,' Harness said. 'This Barrett must be the one Mike had a run-in with before he came to town. Maybe that's why Mike was carryin' his gun arm in a sling. He recognized this Barrett as soon as he stepped outta the back room with Tom, but all Tom did was come up an' talk real nice with him.'

The marshal twisted the crooked cigar around in his mouth. 'Tom's gone soft,' he stated flatly. 'Ever since he—' He shook his head. 'If Cash finds out—'

'Let Cash find out hisself,' Harness warned. 'Don't you tell him.'

Gaines' eyes hardened. 'If Tom eases up too much I'll tell him!' he snapped. 'An' if Cash don't like it—' He rubbed his chin with the knuckles of his right hand and looked squarely at Bull. 'We been doin' most of the dirty work, Bull. Why work for only half the spoils?'

Bull glanced quickly toward the rear of the saloon. Gaines' voice had been low, but Harness was careful. 'If it comes to a break,

I'm with you,' he said softly. 'But don't force it. Not yet.'

Gaines straightened. 'What's this tieup between this new Barrett an' the Brister gal?'

Bull shrugged. 'I don't know. But mebbe it'll turn out for the best, Buck. Charlie Brister will do what we want, and if we have to we can get through to this Barrett through her.'

'I like the direct way myself,' Gains said, scowling. 'If this hardcase gets in our way, I'll take care of him. He won't need much proddin', looks like, an' *I'm* the law here—'

'For how long?' snapped Harness. 'Use yore head, Buck, an' don't let thet tin badge on yore vest blind yuh. Old Pedro Aragon's been too proud to appeal to Houston for an investigation of conditions here. But if we get too raw, someone will write in for the Rangers. We better have our tracks well covered by then.'

Gaines nodded reluctantly. 'Just the same, Bull, I say things are goin' too slow to suit me. I've got the boys ready to raid Aragon beef tomorrow night. If we pull it off right we'll give Pedro an' thet fire-eatin' foreman of his somethin' to get really hoppin' mad over. An' well leave enough evidence around to make 'em head straight for the Cross B!'

Harness nodded grimly. 'Just watch yore step, Buck.'

CHAPTER TEN

Ann Brister toyed with her food. Pablo's, with its thick adobe walls and hardpacked earthen floor, was pleasantly cool, and at this siesta hour they were pretty much alone. The food was good and the red wine went well with it. Their corner table, quiet and not too well lighted, was illumined by a candle set in a hammered copper holder. The flickering light lent an air of intimacy which Ann, who ate here often, had not previously felt.

She was aware, as she listened to Cole talk, of a core of warmth in her that kindled up into a glow, and she pulled her thoughts together long enough to wonder if the flutter within her was something more than a by-product of her loneliness.

It was six months since she had come down to this out-of-the-way village so close to the Mexican border, and she had made few friends. The men her father dealt with had a roughness that only deepened her natural reserve, so that she seemed more unfriendly than was the case. Other than Mrs. Simpson, the wife of the harness maker, who sometimes looked upon her as her ward, Ann had met socially only Martha Barrett and Juanita Aragon. No friendships had struck up between them. The Barrett girl was distantly polite and rarely came to town. She saw Juanita more often, but their relation was rather strained. Outwardly friendly, the Aragon girl occasionally revealed an inner resentment of Ann's presence in town, and it had added to her loneliness.

She did not know all the reasons behind her father's decision to come here. He had been a prominent attorney in Avondale, and as a widower with an only child, he had been socially favored by the town matrons. Quite suddenly Ann learned he had lost all his money on railway stocks, and rumors began to circulate concerning certain shady dealings in which her father had been involved. Ann never learned the details, but her father suddenly began to drink himself to a fast death, and she had welcomed the letter from a 'Mr. Cash Gillis' which had brought them to San Ramos.

It had taken Ann less than two weeks to realize that changing Avondale for San Ramos had not changed things with her father. The knowledge had begun to shrivel her natural self-assurance, and she hadn't realized how close to tears she was until this moment. Seeing this man who had been an officer in the Union Army brought forth a nostalgia for a social life she had tried to forget.

Cole sensed her mood and cut short his recital. 'I guess that's most of it, Ann. I ran away from home to get away from my father and I joined the Union cavalry to get even, I guess.' He looked at her soberly, wondering at the lightness of his mood. This girl was something he had not expected in San Ramos, and he felt her quiet steadiness hold him, like an anchor to his restlessness.

She said: 'All the same I'm glad you were at that ball that night, Cole.' She smiled in remembrance. 'Long ago a top sergeant read my palm and told me I could not escape my destiny.'

Cole laughed. 'And what was your destiny?'

She smiled mischievously. 'I'll tell you some other day.' She pushed her plate aside and reached for her bag. 'Now I must get back to the office. Dad is expecting me.'

Cole got up and left money on the table. Pablo beamed at them from the kitchen doorway. They walked out into the bright sunlight and Ann took his arm. It was the instinctive gesture of a woman used to a different kind of society, and he felt an odd tingle go through him.

'You know,' she confessed shyly, 'San Ramos suddenly looks different. I was beginning to hate its squalidness. But now—'

She stopped and the animation went out of her face, leaving her eyes cool and impersonal. He turned and followed her glance and he saw his sister getting into the wagon in front of Jake's.

Martha ignored them. She settled back in the seat, looked behind her to see if the grocer's boy had secured the last of the supplies in the wagon bed, and drove off.

Ann Brister watched her for a moment before saying softly: 'She hates you, doesn't she?' and Cole didn't say anything, feeling only a gray misery come over him again, robbing the day of its gladness.

They walked on in silence, and at the foot of the flight of stairs leading up to Brister's office, Ann said: 'Thank you for a very pleasant luncheon.'

He said stubbornly: 'I'll see you upstairs, Ann. I want to say hello to your dad.'

Ann turned a startled face to him. 'Not today,' she said quickly. 'Please. He's very busy, and—' she trickled off lamely. 'Please!'

He said: 'All right, then. But I will see you again, soon as I get things straightened out a little at the ranch.' He replaced his hat on his head. 'You know,' he added, smiling, 'I've got a feeling I'm going to be your destiny.'

A wistful smile passed swiftly across Ann's eyes. 'Good-bye,' she said, and turned to the stairs.

He hesitated a moment, feeling unsatisfied and restless, and then he turned away. 'Quit acting like a schoolboy,' he told himself. 'You'll see her again.'

Ann watched him from the window, her slim body pulled back so that she could not be seen from outside. She stood there until Cole Barrett passed out of her sight; then her

86

father's blurred and angry voice pulled her away and she went to him with patient resignation.

'Who you mooning over?' he demanded. 'Who's caught your fancy? One of these bandy-legged louts—'

'Dad!' she cut at him sharply, and a choleric color came into Charles Brister's heavy, puffed face. He was a big man who had been drinking heavily and eating too well for a long time, and it was beginning to take its toll. He had small brown eyes almost hidden behind thick blond brows and heavy pouches. An innate greed for money and power had shaped him so that their loss had been a bitter blow from which he had never recovered. He had come to San Ramos at Cash Gillis' bidding, expecting to share as an equal in the profits ahead, only to realize that he was but to be a pawn—to be used for his respectability and his knowledge of the law when Cash would take over the Cross B and the running of Shadow Valley. He was a front man without real power, and his dream of making enough money to return to Avondale with the financial standing he had once enjoyed had vanished with the passing months.

He hated what he was doing to his daughter and he hated himself, and he took recourse in the bottle and worked out his frustrations against her. And now he suddenly hated her patient resignation . . .

'Damn it, Ann!' he roared, pounding the

table. 'I told you before, get out of San Ramos. Go back to live with your Aunt Katherine, before you sink to the level—'

She interrupted quietly: 'I'll get you some black coffee.' She left him, going through a rear door to living quarters. He stood hunched over the desk, his bloodshot eyes angry, feeling only the heat and the dinginess of this office twisting like a knife inside him . . .

CHAPTER ELEVEN

In front of the Lone Star Saloon, Cole Barrett was thoughtfully getting into the saddle of his waiting mount. Despite its bad beginning the afternoon had worn on pleasantly. Meeting Ann Brister had awakened old memories— touched a lost chord of happiness deep within him.

He recalled Charley Brister now: a big, pompous-looking man who had nodded to him at the officers' ball and then had completely ignored him. Attorney Brister was a socially prominent man in Avondale, and he had not been impressed by a young second lieutenant of Union Cavalry.

But Ann Brister had made up for her father's slight. A gracious girl, she had made Cole feel welcome—helped smooth the rough edges from his new second lieutenant's bars.

Wonder what's brought Charley Brister into this corner of Texas? he mused. Money? Brister was that kind of man, Cole remembered. But what kind of money would bring soft-living Charley Brister here?

He dismissed the speculation, and a corner of his mind remained content with the fact—Ann was in San Ramos, and he would see more of her. He tilted his hat back from his forehead and began to whistle—something he hadn't done in years.

He was turning the gray away from the hitchrack, in toward the center of the dusty street, when the animal suddenly shied away from the path of another rider coming at a gallop from the Mexican section of town. The gray's abrupt move nearly unseated Cole. He curbed the skittish animal with a hard hand and turned angrily to the hasty horseman.

Juanita Aragon's amused glance met his hard regard. *'Buenos dias, estranjero,'* she greeted him. She held her mincing buckskin to a walk and eased him to Cole's side. 'I see you have found your way to San Ramos safely enough?'

He touched his hat brim civilly and swung the gray in beside her. 'Are you disappointed?'

She smiled archly. 'You struck me as being a very capable man, *señor.* I had no fear you would find your way, wherever you wished to go.'

He let a smile come to his lips. 'Carlos'

directions were direct. He left me no chance of a mistake. I hope you found your brother as easily as I found my way here.'

The teasing smile drained from her face. She bit her lips. 'No. Julio has gone away before. But always we knew where he had gone. This time—' she made a little gesture with her hands, as if unconsciously trying to get hold of something, 'this time his disappearance worries us, *señor*.'

'If he's over twenty-one, he's probably found himself a dark-eyed chiquita,' Cole said bluntly. 'Anyway, I hardly think—'

'You do not know Julio,' the girl interrupted coldly. Then, turning her face away, she changed the subject. 'Didn't you find the Cross B to your liking?'

He shrugged. They were nearing the end of town now and the sun was in his face. He tugged his hat brim down to shield his eyes. 'I'll ride with you a piece,' he offered, 'unless you prefer riding alone.'

'If I had preferred it, *señor*,' she smiled teasingly again, 'I would not have stopped to talk with you.' Her eyes, gray and dark, revealed a sudden frankness that caught him unawares. 'You interest me, *señor*. You see, I have not forgotten what happened in El Toro's.'

'I have,' he said shortly. He ran his eyes over her. This slim, well-formed girl broke all the rules of family custom, he thought dryly. She

90

was dressed in velvet green *pantalones* and a yellow silk shirt that matched the tumbled mass of her hair. A fawn-colored jacket rested lightly on her shapely shoulders and a big cream sombrero shaded her face.

She doesn't look Spanish, he thought. She looks anything but Spanish. Most of the Spanish girls he had known were duenna-ridden and close-watched and they rode side-saddle if they rode at all. But he was beginning to suspect that the Aragons were an unusual family—or Miss Aragon was, at least.

'You have not answered me,' Juanita said as they took the south trail at the fork. 'Didn't you find the Cross B hospitable?'

'Not as friendly as I would have liked,' he countered grimly. 'Especially when I rode in with a dead man across my saddle.'

She turned and looked at him, surprise arching the line of her brows. 'A dead man, *señor*?'

He nodded, and the memory hardened his mouth. 'I found Bill Barrett lying under his horse on the Salt Creek trail. He was dead.'

She reined in abruptly, and Cole had to pull the gray to one side to avoid a collision. Juanita's face was strained.

'Bill Barrett?'

Cole repeated it, his tone curious. 'You knew Bill Barrett?'

'Yes.' Her lips went soft and memory drew tiny lines of regret across her brow. She had

91

known Bill better than she wanted to admit, Cole thought.

'A likable boy,' she said, shrugging. 'But a Barrett.'

'You don't like the Barretts?'

She tossed her head, giving her mount a little dig with her heels. 'They are intruders here,' she said coldly. 'The Barretts especially. Making a pretense of ranching while they steal our cattle.'

'You're sure of that, Miss Aragon?' Cole cut in brusquely.

She glanced up at him with some surprise. 'It is what my father believes, and Manuel, our foreman. Even my brother Julio thinks so.'

'Is it what you believe?'

She looked thoughtful. 'I don't know,' she admitted. 'Why? Why are you curious about the Barretts?'

He shrugged.

'Who killed Bill Barrett?'

'Someone who knew he would be on his way back to Cross B from San Ramos,' Cole answered levelly. 'Someone who knew he always took the Salt Bluff trail home. Someone who waited for him on the trail—and killed him with a sword!'

Her eyes widened and he saw fear flicker in them. 'I didn't believe the story they told me at the Cross B,' Cole went on. 'A story of a crazy Mexican in armor who's been running amok in the valley. But someone killed Bill Barrett with a weapon like that!'

She said in a small voice barely audible above the sound of their jogging mounts, 'I have heard the stories, too, *señor*. The villagers say it is the ghost of old Miguel who killed himself long ago.'

'The man who killed Bill Barrett was no ghost, Juanita.'

She reined in on a rise in the road, and off in the distance, tucked in a fold between the low hills, the sun marked the windows of the Aragon hacienda. She turned to him, suddenly curious.

'I waited to see if you would tell me, *señor*. But perhaps you have a reason. You have the advantage of me. You know who I am. But I do not even know your name.'

Cole faced her. 'I'm Cole Barrett,' he said. 'The black sheep of a son, who's come home.'

For a meager moment Juanita Aragon did not move. But her face suddenly grew pinched and a hardness turned her gray eyes to spiteful agates. 'A Barrett!' she said, almost spitting out the words. She reached for the quirt that hung from her pommel.

Cole caught her wrist and pulled her in close. 'You're the second woman who's tried that,' he said harshly. He reached over and took the quirt from her with his free hand.

She was straining to pull free, her face close. Her hat had slipped back on her shoulders and her hair came loose and framed her face with

93

sudden wantonness.

A sudden riotous impulse took hold of Cole. He pulled her close and kissed her. She fought him, clawing with her free hand. Her lips were hard under his, and then they softened, parted, and her hand ceased raking his shoulders and tightened.

He let her go. Tipped out of her saddle, she lost her balance. She made a grab for her pommel and succeeded in sliding down in a sitting position.

Cole reached down and pulled her to her feet. 'Good night,' he said, and touched his hat brim. He left her standing beside her buckskin, raging silently . . .

*   *   *

The range north of the Aragon ranch was dark and empty, and a late rising moon cast an orange glow in the sky over the ragged Pinnacles. A wind blew up from the south, rustling against the spiked growth, and somewhere in the pale darkness a coyote yelped sharply to the warm and yellow stars.

The Pinnacles made a wall up ahead, dark and sombre, and hiding the Cross B ranchhouse within their dark shadows. Hammer Peak was a lesser bulk in the night, and he turned for it, putting the gray to a run. The land ahead sloped away to the dry creek bottoms and the tangled bosque of the Salt

94

Creek ravines where he had had his run-in with Manuel. This was the land of the Aragons whose title went back more than a hundred years. To the Aragons the Barretts were intruders—and thieves.

Cole reviewed events since he had come home. He should have gone up to the Benches to help Barney. For Barney was trying to get a herd together, and cattle meant money. To get those cattle on the trail Barney needed help— needed men willing to work, to risk a dangerous trail.

But it took money to hire men. And the Cross B was broke. The irony of it hit Cole as he jogged through the night, and for a coldly dispassionate moment he considered advising his father to sell the Cross B for what it would bring and to get away from this corner of Texas.

The fire caught his eye, rousing him from his reverie. It was a small blaze in the night, and it plucked at his interest. This was uncertain ground between the Cross B and the Triple A, and he was curious to learn who would be camping out here.

He turned the gray and approached the fire, his senses alert. He rode slowly, keeping to the patches of shadow cast by mesquite. He found himself riding slack and ready, his right hand resting loosely on the rise of saddle. And the thought came to him, with detached amusement, that four wartime years had changed him and trained him to quick suspicion.

The fire was dying down, losing its first bright blaze, when he came within sight of it. He reined in just outside its flickering glow and leaned forward over the horn, a dark figure in the shadows. A battered enameled coffee pot was sitting on a stone on the edge of the blaze. It was simmering, and the pleasant tang of strong brew reached him.

There was no one at the fire.

Cole dismounted, making his motions easy, unhurried. From the darkness to his left a voice chuckled. It was a pleasant, low voice. 'Take a good look, pilgrim.'

Cole turned. The ground dipped sharply to a small wash, and from somewhere within its blackness a horse moved restlessly. Cole faced the shadows. A man moved out of them, came slowly within the flickering red glow.

Surprise moved Cole slightly, ironing out the smile on his face. Even in the shifting light he recognized his double—and the resemblance was marked.

'This must be Calico,' he thought, and interest stirred sharply in him.

The man held a .45 Army Colt in his hand, and his arm hung down by his side so that the muzzle pointed groundward. He halted a few paces away and studied Cole, the wood fire reflected in tiny red glints in his eyes. 'You could, at that!' he remarked softly.

'Could what?'

His teeth were white, and he showed them in a small smile that changed the lines of his dark face, gave it a suddenly boyish cast. 'Could be my brother,' he answered. He shrugged, as if making a thought-out decision, and holstered his Colt.

'What outfit, pilgrim?'

'B Company, 12th Cavalry,' Cole replied.

Calico was reflective for a moment. Cole noticed that he was shabbily dressed, and even the worn and scuffed leather holster and belt that hung low around his waist added nothing to the dangerous reputation associated with him. He looked like a saddle bum, yet there was a quiet dignity in him, too, as though he found the world a sad place not worth living in, but nevertheless had a gentleman's code of duty to make the best of it.

Yet this was the man whose name had shaken Mike to his heels and stopped Manuel, the craggy Triple A foreman!

'I was at Bull Run with the 13th,' Calico said, and waved an inviting hand toward the coffee. 'The joe's hot and black. Join me?'

Cole nodded. He walked to the fire, and the other bent over the pot and poured the black liquid into a tin cup. 'Some men claim it keeps them awake,' he said conversationally, handing Cole the cup. 'With me it acts as a sedative—I sleep like a baby.'

Cole glanced up at the late rising moon. 'A

97

bad practice, I hear, in these parts. Especially when the moon gets like that—'

Calico stopped and looked up at Cole. 'I see you've heard the stories, too. About Miguel's ghost.'

'Ghost, nothing!' Cole said shortly.

Calico's gaze narrowed. But Cole was hunkered down on his heels, sipping the coffee. Calico stepped into the shadows and fumbled in his saddle pack. He came back with another cup. 'Always bring along a spare,' he explained. 'For company.'

Cole watched him. A thought annoyed him. What was a man like this doing here, camping here on this middle ground between the Triple A and the Cross B?

Calico asked: 'Headin' south?'

Cole shook his head. 'I'm staying.' He lifted the cup to his lips again, his eyes meeting Calico's quiet, questioning gaze. He added levelly: 'I'm Cole Barrett.'

The revelation did not particularly disturb the other. 'I heard there was another Barrett,' he said. He got up and started off into the darkness; then he turned and looked down at Cole, and his face, outlined in the dying fire, seemed long and grave. 'The Cross B's done here, fella. It's licked.'

Cole's lips drew back in a tight, half-mocking grin. 'That's a matter of opinion,' he said flatly.

Calico chuckled.

'You settled here?' Cole asked. 'Or passin' on?'

'Settled,' the other answered. 'Why?'

Cole set his empty cup down and straightened. Standing close, they were of a height. But there was more weight in Cole's shoulders, and there was something harder in him, a core of steel more finely tempered. They were remarkably similar, and seen from the back would have been hard to distinguish.

'I'd like to have you on the Cross B,' Cole replied. 'Might be less trying on the nerves.'

Calico arched an eyebrow. He was reaching in his coat pocket for a tailored cigaret, and he offered one to Cole. 'Your nerves don't seem to be giving you trouble.'

Cole chuckled. 'Not mine. But I got into a ruckus with a hot-headed kid named Mike because I looked like you—and later on Aragon's foreman, a craggy gent named Manuel, shied like a spooked bronc when he thought I was you. You seem to have a rep here, fella.'

Calico held a match to Cole's cigaret. 'Manuel and I don't get along,' he admitted.

'Been in Shadow Valley long?'

'Three months. Have a homestead on Salt Creek, up by Mescal Mesa—an old goatherd named Hernandez had built a shack there. I bought him out.' He waved an arm toward the dark hills. 'Both Manuel and Saber tried to run me out.' He smiled faintly.

Cole nodded understandingly. 'Time I was riding.' He held out his hand. 'You're welcome to ride home with me.'

'Thanks. But I like to sleep out. Habit.' His eyes met Cole's with a level regard. 'I have a problem I want to straighten out. Something between me and—' He glanced up at the large yellow stars, and Cole saw his face tighten and a nerve jumped under Calico's right eye.

'Calico's an odd name,' Cole remarked softly. 'If you should change your mind, come in to the Cross B. I'll be glad to see you.'

The other turned. 'The name's John Carlson,' he said quietly. 'And I might take you up on that, Cole—soon.'

He remained by the embers as Cole went back to the gray. Cole waved briefly. '*Adios.*'

Calico nodded. 'Ride easy, Cole,' he said softly.

CHAPTER TWELVE

Cole arrived at the Cross B after midnight. The moon painted the yard and buildings with a soft, deceiving light. Cole rode in under the adobe arch. A shadow moved along the stables and a faint clink of metal whispered in the night.

He reined in and looked across the empty yard to the dark and silent ranchhouse. Its low

100

outlines were softened by the moonglow, and past the stables and the corral the acequia made a soft, cool murmuring.

There was peace here, and beauty—and Cole felt the need in him grow and take firm root. He was through wandering. He had come home. This was home—and here he would stay. And neither Saber nor the Triple A would drive him out.

His thoughts went back to the man he had left standing by the fire—the shabbily dressed man who had called himself John Carlson. A man with a cultured Eastern voice—who looked so much like himself. A man reckoned as dangerous by some of the most dangerous men in the valley.

Some things didn't make sense. Not unless one figured John Carlson as having come to Shadow Valley for a particular reason. What reason? Baldy had said Miguel's ghost rode when the moon was full. Was John Carlson Miguel's ghost? What had he been doing, camping out on the middle ground between the Triple A and the Cross B?

Cole mused irritatedly. He would see Barney first thing in the morning, get the full plight of the Cross B from him. The solution was to get a herd on the trail and to market. That would put the Cross B back on its feet.

He rode to the corral and dismounted. The animal blew sleepily and he patted its warm flank, whispering to him as he stripped his saddle and blankets from the animal. Opening the pole gate, he turned his horse inside, closed the gate and picked up saddle and blankets.

A window closed softly in the night.

He was walking to the harness shop, carrying his saddle, and the sound caught him and pulled him around. The ranchhouse wall facing him was dark with creeping honeysuckle and wild grape. His father's window faced the yard, and upstairs Martha's room opened up to a small iron-railed porch.

Had Martha been watching him?

He shifted the weight of his saddle to his left hand and started through the dark doorway of the harness shop. A faint flicker of light glowed against the panes of his father's windows. Cole caught it through the corner of his eye and he spun around in a startled motion. His foot caught the trailing edge of his blanket at that same moment and he stumbled.

The mishap saved his life!

He heard the deadly whisper of a thrown object over his head—heard it skitter with metallic sound across the beaten earth yard. Warning shocked his nerves to alertness. He dropped blankets and saddle and lunged up, ramming his bulk into the shadow plunging toward him. His shoulder slammed into an iron-sheathed torso and the impact sent the other reeling back. Cole's shoulder numbed.

From the darkness of the harness shop a

man's voice snarled a string of Spanish curses. A sword clanked thinly. But it was a Colt the intruder used.

The gunflare partially lit up a cloaked, armored figure—revealed him indistinctly and briefly. The bullet flicked cloth from Cole's right arm, Then the darkness closed down again and Cole closed in with the man. He forgot his own weapon in the sudden rush of anger overcoming him and remembered only that this man was the killer who had murdered Bill.

His fingers closed on the man's shoulders, dug against chest armor. The prowler's knee caught him in the stomach and dropped him. He let the man's gun arm swing down and his upthrown hand broke the shock of the blow. He rolled erect, still gasping for air, and drove a hand into the dark figure's face. The other's Colt went off accidentally this time, splintering through the wooden wall, and Cole kicked the gun out of his hand. His eyes were now accustomed to the gloom, but he didn't quite see the other's knee, catching him again in the side.

He fell to his knees, and a vicious kick, only partially blocked, knocked him sidewise. The prowler was through the doorway, into the yard.

Cole lunged to his feet. The swordsman of Shadow Valley was crossing the yard, a strangely sinister figure in the moonlight. He looked incredibly tall and unreal as he ran with amazing speed, dark cloak flapping like some enormous wing, moonlight glinting from his armor.

Cole drew his Colt. He leaned dizzily against the door as he brought the weapon up. The intruder reached the corral and had his hands on the pole bars when Cole fired.

The figure recoiled. He pulled his left hand in toward his body in an instinctive gesture of pain. Cole fired again as the man gave up the idea of hurdling the corral and started to run for the clump of cottonwoods shadowing the well. He ran in zigzag fashion, and he seemed to have wings on his feet. Cole wasted one more long shot. But the killer passed into the concealing shadows and was gone.

Cole started after him. His breathing was still labored. He was almost at the corral when he caught the bright glare of fire from the house!

Cole turned back. Flames werc dancing behind the glass of his father's bedroom windows. The rest of the house was dark and silent.

Cole hurdled the vine-covered veranda railing and plunged into the house. The faint odor of smoke was in the big living room. He ran down the corridor to his father's room. The door was closed. He put his shoulder to it and slammed it open.

Smoke burned his eyes. It lay thick along

the ceiling. The flames, climbing like shifting red imps along the sides of the casement windows, revealed a figure sprawled limply across the foot of the bed.

Cole pulled the covers off the bed and beat out the flames. The adobe walls had not offered too much fuel to the flames, but the danger of asphyxiation by smoke was still imminent. He threw open the windows and the cool night air made him cough. He took several deep breaths into his aching lungs and turned back to the figure across the foot of the bed.

Martha came into the room then, holding a single wax taper in a silver candlestick. Behind her shuffled Ah Ling, an incongruously comical figure in flannel nightgown and stocking cap.

The candle flickered wildly in the draft between door and window. Martha was dressed in an old flannel wrapper, her long hair made up into two braids, tied at their ends with red cotton strips. She looked like a little girl, her face softened by the candlelight—a little girl tiptoeing into her father's room. But Cole noticed that her eyes were hard and alert, and not the eyes of a person just roused from sleep.

The implication of that held him for a moment so that he stared at her.

Martha's gaze shifted to the dresser where a half-empty bottle of whiskey stood. 'He's getting as bad as Barney. Has to go to bed with a bottle.'

Cole turned away from her, stifling the enormity of his suspicion. His father was lying across the counterpane, breathing stertorously. One gnarled hand trailed, fist closed, down almost to the floor. His eyes were closed and blood trickled from a nasty head blow that had laid his scalp wide open just above his left eye.

Cole turned him over and pulled him back upon the pillow. The smoke had thinned out, but the acrid odor of scorched cloth hung in the room. Down between the dresser and the window lay the shattered fragments of an oil lamp, and Cole, looking at it, surmised that the killer must have smashed it to start the fire.

Martha stood in the doorway, making no move to help him. She watched Cole straighten her father out on the bed. Cole snapped: 'Ling—get some hot water and bandages!'

Ling nodded and shuffled off.

'Is he dying?' Martha asked.

Cole turned to her. 'We'll talk about that later—after we've done what we can for him. Or don't you care?'

She smiled—a strange, cold smile. 'Just for the record—no!'

Her indifference shocked him. He crossed the room and grasped her roughly by the shoulders. 'What's gotten into you, Martha? What's happened to you—to all of you?'

She looked up into his face, smiling, making no move to pull away, making no sign that he was hurting her. 'What do you think this is going to get you?' she asked harshly. 'Since you've showed up you've acted like "I'll-take-care-of-things-Cole." Who do you think you are?'

He let her go, feeling the hate in her strained voice.

'It's time you learned. Bill's dead. Barney is through. Paw—' Her eyes went to the badly hurt man on the bed and she shrugged indifferently. 'What do you think you can do? Why? You ran away, eight years ago. Why did you come back? No one wants you here—'

'Paw does,' Cole reminded her grimly.

'Paw doesn't know his own mind any more. And he's better off dead!' she added callously.

'Someone tried to do just that,' he said, holding himself in. He remembered the sound of windows closing when he had ridden in. Martha's windows?

'You sure?' she snapped. 'Or did Paw have one drink too many and knock the lamp off the dresser himself before falling on the bed?'

'You don't believe that?' he asked angrily. 'Who are you covering up for? Miguel's ghost?'

She started, her eyes widening a little as if he had hurt her. 'You don't mean to say you believe that story?' she said, and her lips curled. 'Not Cole Barrett!'

107

Either she knew what he meant and was covering up admirably, or— He turned away from her, feeling helpless against her hate, her indifference to what had happened to Marcus. He took the whiskey bottle from the dresser and turned back to the bed. Marcus lay as he had been placed. His breathing was shallow, rasping. All the long, hard years seemed to have engraved themselves in furrows on his face, and the lines cutting down from the corners of his mouth stamped his whole expression with grim and futile finality. For forty years he had ridden roughshod over his family and it was paying off now in the disunity of his offspring, in their indifference.

There was little left except the blood tie between Cole and his family. He hadn't helped his father by running away—and now that he was back, he intended seeing this crisis through. Some quirk in Cole reacted to the challenge facing him, to the heavy sense of defeat that lay like an inexorable weight over the Cross B.

He slid an arm under his father's limp head and raised it. Martha watched him. She made no move to help. He poured some whiskey from the bottle into Marcus' partially open mouth. Some of it spilled onto Marcus' striped nightshirt.

The old man gagged. A weak cough wracked him. But his eyes remained closed. He groaned softly.

Cole eased him down.

Martha said: 'We're through here. The sooner you realize that, and leave, the better for all of us!'

Ah Ling appeared behind her with a basin of water and bandages. She stepped aside to let him enter. Her eyes were dark and uncompromising. 'There's nothing you can do!'

He watched her leave. The silver moonlight made a bar of light across the rumpled bed. Ah Ling found a match and lighted the tapers on the heavy oaken dresser. The Chinaman was shaking his head.

'Martha fight all the time, Master Cole. She fight with Barney, with Bill, with Mister Marcus. She is a very unhappy girl, that Martha . . .'

Marcus' condition remained unchanged during the night. Cole sat up with his father until Ah Ling came in and insisted on relieving the watch. He went to his room and lay fully clothed across the bed and fell asleep almost immediately.

The sun was breaking through massed horizon clouds when he awoke. Ah Ling brought him coffee, black and strong, and it cleared away some of the fog from his mind.

Ah Ling reported that Marcus was still unconscious, and that Miss Martha had not come out of her room yet.

Cole said: 'I'm going to town for the doctor,

Ling. Its the only thing we can do.'

Ling wrung his hands. His old, yellow-gray face showed the strain of what had happened. 'I will tell Martha,' he said.

Cole washed himself. His jaw was dark with stubble and his eyes were red-rimmed. He went out afterward to the harness shop, and the remembrance of the armored figure who had waylaid him here brought a bitter twist to his lips. Did Martha know? Was she shielding someone?

His blanket and saddle lay on the floor, just as he had dropped them last night. To one side, under a sawhorse, he found the prowler's Colt. It was an ordinary sixgun with a walnut grip, the plates worn smooth by much handling.

Coming across the yard toward the corral he picked up a knife—a woodsman's blade with a horn handle. This was what he had ducked last night.

The gray was rested and lively. He saddled and rode out of the yard, under the adobe arch. He didn't look back, even though he felt he was being watched, by Martha perhaps.

He headed down the trail for San Ramos. The sun was beginning to simmer the air in the draws. He felt its warmth on his shoulders, and ten minutes of riding brought the sweat out under his arms. It seemed to loosen him up, to melt the stiffness from his mind.

Four miles from the Cross B a rider cut

110

down a sandy slope to intercept him. Cole reined in and watched the man ride toward him—a lean, casual rider with a low-hanging gun.

Calico!

He nodded, greeting him as Calico raised his right hand to him. He had a cigarette between his lips. 'I was headed your way,' he said. His keen glance took in Cole's tired features. 'You look done in, fella.'

'Some,' Cole admitted. 'I'm headed to town for a doctor. Is there one in San Ramos?'

Calico nodded. 'Smelt's a good man, too—though I can't imagine what he's doing down here. Did someone get hurt?'

Cole's eyes rested on the blue bandanna that was wrapped around Calico's left hand. He said tightly: 'Yeah, my father.' He clipped off the details of what had happened during the night.

Calico was frowning. 'So you ran into Miguel's ghost, eh? You know I always thought that someone was putting it on pretty thick. But if you say you ran into the jasper, then I believe you.'

Cole's eyes were still on Calico's bandaged left hand. The lanky rider smiled. 'Cut it on a can of peaches I opened this morning,' he explained.

Cole said coldly: 'Sure it wasn't a lug?'

'Sure.' Calico shrugged. 'You look beat, Cole. Let me ride to town for Doc Smelt—I

111

want him to take a look at this cut, anyway. And'—he hesitated a bare instant—'I've got business here that I've decided to settle.'

Cole hesitated. He looked into Calico's serious face. Could this be the man he had encountered last night? Was Calico playing a game here in the valley?

The other was saying cheerfully: 'I thought about that job you offered me last night. If it's still open, I'll take it.'

Cole said tightly: 'Pay's on promise. And you might have to rustle up your own grub. But if you stick—'

'I've rustled my grub before,' Calico said, grinning wryly. 'And I'll stick. I expect to stay in this valley a long time—settle here.' He held out his right hand. 'Then it's a deal!'

Cole took the man's hand. He had to trust somebody in this cockeyed setup. Cole watched him as he swung off toward town.

Calico's explanation about his hand had seemed so ready and slick. He could have been the man who had come to the Cross B last night.

Cole shrugged. He swung the gray around and rode back to the ranch. He came to the road cutting under the adobe arch in time to see Barney Barrett and Hank jog through the opening. Something in the way big Barney sat his horse told Cole that his brother was through . . .

With a growing sense of disaster he spurred

112

the gray ahead to meet them.

CHAPTER THIRTEEN

The war had robbed Barney Barrett. Not of health or of looks—in these he was the same man who had ridden off with the Texas Volunteers, that cocksure regiment that was so certain it would drive the Yankees into the sea. He still stood six feet one in his stocking feet and the years had made him harder, if anything. He was blond and his face was good-looking in a rugged, masculine way. But the old Barney who used to laugh with infectious humor at just plain living, the big man with the natural good nature was dead.

Somewhere along the dark and bloody years between Fort Sumter and Appomattox, Barney had lost something of himself. It was there in his face for anyone to read, there in the surly nod he gave Cole now, as they met.

His features, coarser under a heavy blond stubble, were still strong. But there was a slackness to his mouth that Cole could not remember. And his heavy drinking was pushing tiny red veins to the surface of his cheeks, giving him a dissipated look. He rode slackly in the saddle, shoulders hunching forward. There was a truculent surliness in his eyes as he turned in the saddle and watched

113

Cole draw alongside.

'Hank told me you had showed up,' he greeted him. He shook Cole's hand with a restrained gesture—but the old Barney would have thrown an arm around Cole and roared out his pleasure. Long ago Barney had understood why Cole had left.

Now he let his bloodshot eyes run down the yellow stripe of Cole's trousers, and he spat his deliberate disapproval.

'It's good to see you again, Barney,' Cole told him.

Then a silence fell between them, weighted with the barrier of the years. There was nothing between them, and they both knew it.

Martha's words came to beat harshly in Cole's ears. *Barney's through. We're all through here. And the sooner you know this, the better it will be!*

Cole tried to recapture something of the old feeling for his brother. 'I'm glad to be home,' he said, breaking the awkward silence.

Barney shrugged. 'There's not much left, kid.' His voice was flat, with neither bitterness nor anger—both these emotions seemed to have gone out of Barney. 'Hank told me about Bill,' he continued. 'If he had stayed up on the Benches with me, he'd probably be alive today.'

Cole's lips tightened. 'He was riding home, minding his own business, Barney, and someone killed him. I don't know who it was, or why—but Bill was my brother—and yours. What are we going to do about it, Barney? Sit here and say he should have been up on the Benches with you?'

Barney scowled.

Hank edged in, trying to relieve the gathering tension. 'You look done in, Cole. Something happened?'

Cole nodded. 'We had trouble last night,' he said. 'The same man who killed Bill slugged Paw last night, and tried to burn the house down. Paw's in a bad way. I started out to get a doc for him when I saw you coming in.'

Barney's eyebrows raised. 'Reckon you ain't the only one had trouble last night,' he said dryly. 'We were raided again. Potley got killed. The others quit.' He rubbed the bristle on his jaw. 'This is what's left of the Cross B, kid. Hank and me.'

Hank said with patient resignation: 'Two months' work gone for nothing, Cole. Them cattle are spooked all over the Benches, and they'll be harder than 'Paches to round up again. It's gonna be one devil of a job to round 'em up, even if we get another crew together—'

Cole snapped: 'You quitting, too?'

Hank looked hurt.

Barney said: 'Don't be so blamed touchy, kid! Why shouldn't Hank quit? We owe him six months' wages. We can't pay him—and it looks like we never will. We're through here, Cole—and we might as well face it!'

Cole looked at his brother, understanding of him tempering the hot anger crawling through him. Barney was right. What did they have to fight with?

Hank suggested quietly: 'Let's go on in and take a look at Marcus. And then after some of Ling's grub an' coffee, mebbe we'll all feel a whole lot better.'

*   *   *

Barney stood beside his father's bed. Twenty years ago his father had looked like this, big, blond and hard—but age had come quickly upon Marcus after his injury, and now there was little resemblance between him and his oldest boy. Between Marcus and his son there had always existed a bond—the unconscious bond which exists between a father and his first son.

Barney stood awkwardly by the bedstead now, his big hands clenching and unclenching on his hat. Then he caught Cole's look and asked him: 'The doc on his way?' Cole nodded, trusting Calico.

They walked back to the dining room, where Ah Ling was serving coffee. Hank said: 'I'll give Ling a hand in the kitchen, Barney.' He walked off.

Barney sat moodily over his coffee. Cole paced the room, trying for an answer to the problem facing the Cross B. Wanting so much

116

to reach to this beaten brother of his in the chair.

'What sort of man is Pedro Aragon?' he asked.

Barney looked up at him. 'Met him twice, kid. From what I hear, he's as proud as Lucifer. Thinks the Aragons should own all of the valley—by divine right. But 'e's a decent sort, I guess, in his own way.'

Cole remembered Juanita's outburst just before they had parted. 'But he hates the Barretts. Why?'

Barney shrugged. 'All right, kid—this is the way it goes. We bought out young de Gama, and we inherited the dislike that existed between the de Gamas and the Aragons. That's one reason. The other reason is that our land adjoins the Triple A. Now old Pedro Aragon's losing stock—from what I hear, some of the stuff is blooded stock that he's been trying to improve. I know Saber's behind the rustling—with help from the town crowd. But Pedro's unaware of it. Saber is way out in the Pinnacles. We're close—and he thinks we're intruders anyway. So . . .'

'So it's time we got out!' Martha added coolly. She had come into the dining room without being heard. She stood there looking at them, her face strained and white. Martha was a tall girl, and her Levis and blue chambray shirt did not detract from the appeal of her full figure. She could have been pretty, but she was hard.

Barney did not even look at her. He eased back in his chair and started to roll a smoke.

Cole asked: 'Why? Because old Aragon's pushing us?' He turned to Barney. 'Who was behind last night's raid? Was it Aragon's men?'

'I recognized one of the town bunch that hang around the "Lone Star," and I'd say Saber was behind it.' Barney's voice sounded suddenly flat as he looked at Martha for the first time since she had come into the room. 'Cash Gillis has made no secret of the fact that he's out to break us—'

Martha's lips curled. 'What does it matter whether it was Saber or the Triple A behind the raid? The main thing is that we're through here!' She said it scornfully, and watching her, Cole had a sudden insight into her motives. All her life Martha had been dominated by the men in her family. And now, although perhaps she was unaware of it herself, she was hitting back at them all . . . Nothing would change Martha's attitude. Cole knew that now. Perhaps Barney would listen to reason. Perhaps he could see that there was a way out.

'It matters a lot,' he said evenly. 'We've got one chance—our only chance. Saber's been playing a smart game. They've got us in the middle and they're breaking us. But if we can get Pedro Aragon to see that it is Saber that's behind these cattle raids, we can turn the tables on them. We'll do it without men,

118

Barney—we'll do it with Aragon riders!'

Barney was grinning now, a faint ghost of his old spirit showing in his eyes. Martha came to them at the table.

'Listen, Cole! Paw will probably be dead before morning. That leaves Barney and me in charge here—you don't count! You don't count here, Cole, you hear!' Her voice was rasping and choked with the intensity of her hatred. 'And I say you're not wanted here. I never wanted you back! You and all the other yellowlegs who killed Johnny Vickers. I'll never forget that! Never, never!'

Cole kept silence. He glanced at Barney. His brother's eyes were narrowed in a quizzical look. 'Mebbe I'd likc to see Cole stay, Martha,' he told her softly. 'At least he's for the Cross B. As far as I'm concerned, the war's over.'

Martha spun around to him, her eyes venomous and blazing. She gripped the table. 'Barney—either Cole goes, or I go! I won't live in the same house with him!'

'Cole stays!'

Her face became livid. She straightened up. 'You fool!' she said softly. She turned on her heels and strode out.

Barney looked up at Cole. Martha's tongue-lashing hadn't impressed him much, it seemed. 'I don't believe we can do it, kid. But I'm willing to give it one more try. Mebbe we owe it to the old man, eh?'

119

*   *   *

John Carlson, alias Calico, jogged into San Ramos at noon. The hot sun beat down over the squalid structures, driving most of its inhabitants to the comparative coolness of indoors. A few half-breed Mexicans squatted with their backs to the adobe walls, half-dozing in the shade of their sombreros.

Passing the 'Lone Star,' Calico noticed Buck Gaines lounging in his chair, hat pulled low over his eyes, a dead cheroot dangling from the corner of his mouth. Dust dulled the marshal's badge on his vest.

Gaines didn't move. But Calico knew that he was being watched. He rode past and turned east at the first corner. Doc Smelt had his office in the next block.

He got stiffly out of the saddle and walked up the narrow flight of wooden steps to the doctor's office. The cut on his hand felt stiff now as he tried to work his fingers. He sure could stand having it looked after.

The doctor was out. Calico came down the stairs and stood on the boardwalk, rocking on his heels. He had promised Cole he'd bring the doc out with him, and he wanted to keep his word.

His eyes picked up Attorney Charles Brister's sign down the street, and he came down off his toes. Behind him a voice asked

120

conversationally: 'You looking for the doc?'

Calico turned. The man who had come to the barbershop door was in shirtsleeves. He wiped sweat from his high forehead. 'He just left on a hurry call. Up to Lawyer Blister's office.'

Calico nodded. 'Thanks.' He walked up the street, leading his horse. He had come a thousand miles to meet Blister face to face. His pace quickened.

Ann Brister opened the door at his knock. She looked tired. Her greeting was dubious.

'Hello.'

He took off his hat and stood in the doorway—a tall, serious-faced man in a dusty shirt. He glanced past her, into the room where a short, paunchy man was just closing a black leather bag. Charley Brister lay slumped back in his chair, his eyes closed.

'I'm sorry,' Ann began, 'but if you came to see my father, you'll have to come back some other time. He's not well—'

'I've come for Doctor Smelt,' Calico said. 'A friend of mine has been hurt.'

'Oh—do come in! The doctor was just leaving—'

He stepped inside. Brister opened his eyes to look at the newcomer. A little tremor quivered his heavy jowls. He sat up in his chair with such an abrupt movement that the paunchy medico turned to him.

'You better lay back and take things easy,'

121

Doctor Smelt warned. 'And lay off the bottle, or the next time your heart acts up it will be your last.'

Brister was staring at Calico, not listening to this advice. Ann went up to him. 'Dad—he just wants to see Doctor Smelt.' She turned to Calico. 'Isn't that right?'

Calico nodded. 'I've just come from the Cross B, Doc. Marcus Barrett had an accident. Has a skull fracture, most likely. I think he needs your help—right away.'

The doctor shrugged. 'We'll see what we can do, son.' He turned to Ann. 'See that he takes those pills—one every three hours, in water.' He reached for his hat up on the clothes horse and put it on.

Brister called to him: 'The devil with Marcus Barrett, Doc. You stick around town— I may need you. I don't feel too well right now.'

The doctor merely looked at him, his face immobile but the contempt he felt showing in his mild eyes.

Ann gasped at this and recoiled. 'Father!'

Doctor Smelt went to the door. 'I'll get the buggy hitched and meet you on the trail,' he said to Calico. Then, turning to Ann, he added: 'I'll be back in the morning.' He left the office.

Charley Brister wet his lips. He looked at Ann, then at Calico, his mouth working. Then he blustered: 'You're Calico!' Ann, horror at

122

her father's callousness still on her face, looked at the stranger curiously, then again at her father.

Brister continued: 'I've heard about you. A drifter, and handy with the gun. What's your game here in San Ramos? What are the Barretts to you?'

Calico shrugged. 'Nothing.' He walked up to the desk and looked down at the heavy man. 'Calico's a convenient name that one of the Saber riders tacked onto me. I have another, too. Want to know what it is?'

Brister seemed to shrink back in his chair. His ruddy face went pasty. After a pause he asked: 'Who are you?'

'The name's Carlson!' Calico told him, very softly and very clearly. 'John Carlson.'

He then turned toward Ann, his face serious. 'Sorry I intruded, Miss Brister.' They watched him as he walked to the door and quietly left them, the only sound being the clicking of the door.

Ann was staring at her father, reading terror in his face, and she wondered. She had just remembered that her mother's maiden name had also been Carlson—Amy Carlson!

CHAPTER FOURTEEN

The Saber rider swaggered out to the Lone Star porch, took a hard-boiled hitch at his sagging guns, and bared his yellow buck teeth in a nervous grin. Buck Grimes was in his usual position on the saloon porch, slouched back in his chair, seemingly doing nothing, but missing little that went on within his range of vision.

He glanced up now as Cimarron spat deliberately into the street. Cimarron was a newcomer to the Saber outfit—a toughie from the Territory with a pretty sizeable reward dogging his trail. Gaines, a hard man himself, hadn't taken to Cimarron. But it was Cash who ran the show up at Saber . . .

Cimarron's voice rasped with contempt. 'I tell you, Buck, this Calico jasper is overrated. And I'm gonna prove it.'

Gaines grunted. 'Yo're a damn fool. But go ahead—we'll bury you, anyway.'

Cimarron sneered. He pulled a sack of Durham from his pocket and fashioned a brown paper quirley. 'I figgered you for a pretty craggy customer, Buck. But a saddle bum with a Boston accent comes into the valley, squats under the nose of Saber, and everyone from Cash Gillis on down to you begins to make wild circles. Why? He wears a

124

gun, sure. I wear two, Buck. And I say I kin put five slugs into him before he kin clear leather—'

'I always said you had a big mouth,' the town marshal cut in bluntly. 'But it's yore play. He's comin' out now—down from Brister's office.'

Cimarron took a long drag on the cigarette. He was a narrow-shouldered, wiry man with an habitual squint in his blue eyes. He was only twenty-two, but he had started his career early. He had killed his stepfather with a pitchfork when he was fourteen. It had been an argument over the amount of hay that made a wagonload. There was a mean, vicious streak in him, and subsequent killings had fed a warped ego until now he fancied himself pretty nearly unbeatable.

He had boasted around the Saber bunkhouse how much he would like to match guns with Calico, and here was his chance. He had been in the Lone Star when Calico had come to town, and one of the hardcases inside, remembering his boast, had pointed out that Cimarron would never have a better chance than at this moment to back his big talk.

He watched Calico come down the stairs and he felt Gaines' regard on him. Boots scuffed the floor inside the Lone Star as men moved toward the windows.

Satisfaction twisted a smile on his brown

face. He had his audience, and the show was his.

'Watch this, Buck,' he boasted softly, with a vast amount of arrogance; 'get a good look at some fancy shooting.' He tossed his limp quirley into the dust, and stepped down from the saloon porch . . .

Calico came down the stairs into the bright sunlight of the street. He pulled his hat brim down lower over his eyes and paused on the boardwalk. Charles Brister would remember the name of Carlson. He would sit there and remember—and fear would eat out his soul.

He'd let him wait. He had waited ten years for this moment—since his father's death. All the years of his boyhood he had watched as his father died slowly, a beaten man, broken in spirit. He wanted Charley Brister to remember . . .

The voice across the street was sharply arrogant. 'You goin' somewhere, Calico?'

Calico swung around, pulled back from the bitterness of past memories to the suddenly threatening present. He recognized the man across the street as a Saber man called Cimarron. He was standing on the edge of the boardwalk, the width of the sun-beaten street between them, and Calico recognized the signs at once. The man was out to force a fight and the pattern was set. Back up the street Buck Gaines was standing up on the Lone Star porch, watching . . .

126

Calico's eyes roved down the few yards to where he had left his horse. He didn't want trouble, not this kind of trouble. He had no quarrel with Saber—yet! He had a job to do here, a vengeance that had shaped his life for ten years, driven him from army post to army post looking for a man his father had mentioned with his dying breath.

He forced a smile to his lips. 'Mebbe we both need a drink, feller. Care to join me?'

Cimarron shook his head. Those fools crowding the windows of the Lone Star thought this man was dangerous! Calico was yellow! He was backing down . . .

He raised his voice purposely so that Buck and the others could hear him. 'I don't drink with damn Yankees!' He stepped down into the dust and started to walk toward the other. 'You got a tall name in these parts, Calico. But you don't make big tracks with me. I think yo're yeller—an' I'm gonna prove it.'

Calico's smile settled hard on his lips. There'll be no evading this braggart, he thought. And up the street, at town's end, Doc Smelt would be waiting for him . . .

Calico walked deliberately to his cayuse, ignoring the other who stopped, feet planted wide in the dust. He hooked a leg across saddle and was gathering up the reins when Cimarron's voice snapped:

'Get down off that cayuse!'

Calico swung the bronc around and looked

127

down at the man facing him. The sun was hot on his back, and in the stillness he heard a child wail, and the sound seemed to make this scene unrealistic and meaningless. But there was no evading the man standing in the street.

Calico said impatiently: 'Get out of my way, fella.'

Cimarron's voice was flat. 'Then I guess I'll have to shoot you out of—' He drew as Calico touched his heels to his bronc's flanks. He flipped his right Colt out in a smooth, flashy draw, his buck teeth gleaming in his dark face.

Calico's horse shied nervously at the gun blast close to his face. Calico fought it down with a hard left hand. The reins cut through his bandanna-wrapped palm, opening his cut, drawing blood.

Cimarron was sagging slowly, falling to his knees. His grin was twisted into a warped leer. He had never even fired the gun in his hand.

Calico rode slowly past him. He drew past the Lone Star, his Colt in his hand, his eyes hard, holding the men crowding the porch.

Buck Gaines was scowling. But no one moved. Behind him the street was deserted, hot and empty, except for the body of the dead Saber rider lying motionless in the dust . . .

Doc Smelt was waiting for him at the fork when he drew up by the buggy. The doctor's small, tired eyes searched Calico's dark, impassive face.

'Someone get hurt?'

Calico shrugged. 'A man named Cimarron.' He smiled wryly as the doctor turned to look back toward town. 'He won't be needing you, Doc. Not a-tall.'

*　　　*　　　*

Cole met them in the Cross B ranchyard. Calico nodded to Barney waiting on the steps, and stayed behind while the doctor and Cole went inside.

Barney sat in a wicker chair, staring moodily out across the yard—he conveyed to Calico an impression of silent waiting. As if he didn't care what happened here, but as if he were willing to see how it would all turn out anyway . . .

Calico sat on the railing, knowing he was a stranger here. He let Barney alone. He had his own problem, and the Cross B's problems concerned him little. He had accepted Cole's offer of a job because he had liked what he saw in the man. But he had not known how badly off the Cross B was.

Close up, the deterioration was vividly seen. From sagging sheds to rusted blacksmith tools in the smithy, the atmosphere was that of a run-down spread. Slowly he built himself a smoke.

Doctor Smelt preceded Cole out of the house. He paused and looked at Barney, and his words were as much for his benefit as for

129

Cole's. 'As I said, it looks to me like a gun did that to your father. It's a bad concussion. He may never come out of it. All I can recommend is that you follow my directions. Keep him quiet and have someone stay with him at all times.'

He nodded briefly and went down the steps on to his waiting buggy. Cole watched him pass under the adobe gateway and then turned to Calico.

'Thanks for getting him here, Calico.'

Calico shrugged. Barney turned his sour gaze on them. 'Well, kid, what now? We sit here and wait for Paw to die—'

'We're getting off our butts and starting to do something,' Cole cut in coldly. 'We might as well get this straight, Barney. This morning, when you sided with me against Martha, I figured you were going to fight. Are you?'

Barney flushed. 'Fight with what?' He got to his feet, his hand arcing out in an impatient gesture. 'There's Hank, me and you—'

'And Calico here,' Cole added. 'He's working for us,'

Barney's eyebrows formed amused V's. 'So,' he said slowly. 'A gun-handy drifter. We gonna beat Saber—'

'We're going to try,' Cole interrupted flatly. 'Maybe we're not through yet. Cash Gillis asked me to drop in at Saber, the first time I met him. I'm going to take him up on that. I'm going to try to bargain with him.'

Barney's grin was broad and skeptical. 'Bargain with what?'

'We'll pay him two dollars a head to make the drive through the Pinnacles.' His voice was tight. 'I'll back down on that point if I have to, Barney.'

Barney shook his head. 'Cash won't bargain, kid. I tried.'

Cole looked at Calico, lounging on the railing. 'You want to ride with me to Saber?'

Calico shrugged. 'You're the boss, Cole.'

Cole nodded. 'There's more than one way to skin a cat, Barney,' he said grimly. 'If Cash won't bargain, then we'll try Pedro Aragon.'

Barney grunted. 'Luck to you, kid.'

*   *   *

They left the Cross B early the next morning. The sun was banked under the horizon clouds and the coolness of the night still lingered over the land.

They took an old goat trail west, and Calico led the way—the way to Saber led past his shack on the upper reaches of Salt Creek, so that he was familiar with this part of the valley.

They made the foothills before the sun grew unbearable. Small *piñon* clumps dotting the bare, parched hills relieved the heat. This end of the valley was dry and stony, and Cole understood why Cash Gillis was willing to use any means to break the Cross B. Backed up into this arid fringe of the valley, Saber would never be anything more than a third-rate spread. But Gillis had one joker in his possession—Horsethief Pass.

This was the short way through the Pinnacles—the only way cattle could be driven out of Shadow Valley to the northern markets. And Saber held Horsethief Pass.

They topped a low hogback and reined in to give their animals a blow. Calico pointed to a gash in the foothills. 'The Bueno Padre River goes through there and cuts over behind the Cross B, further down the valley. There's a rough trail through the canyon, but if you're ever in a hurry to get back, that's the short way, Cole.'

Cole nodded.

Behind them the valley opened up, a green and fertile land with the bosque lining the Salt making a dark green boundary, cutting the valley in two, dividing the Cross B from the Triple A. Land enough for both, and grass enough to graze ten times the cattle the Cross B owned.

Run down as it was, that spread was still a prize—and Cole could see that clearly now—a prize worth fighting for.

He turned and caught Calico staring down-valley with an absent look, and he felt the other's indrawn mood. There was something on Calico's mind—it had been there the first time they had met, by the campfire close to the

Salt.

'It ain't any of my business,' Cole told him bluntly, 'but what's a man like you doing in Shadow Valley? You're no farmer.'

Calico shrugged. 'I was educated at Harvard—trained to be a lawyer.'

Cole grinned. 'They teach you how to handle that Colt at Harvard—or is the practice of law that dangerous back East?'

'I learned to use this Colt in the Army,' Calico smiled. 'Came easy—and it fitted my plans.' He was silent then, and so Cole did not prod him.

'I've been looking for a man since I was nineteen,' he continued slowly. 'To kill him.' He put his hands on his saddle and leaned on them, his eyes meeting Cole's. 'I was trained in the law—but what this man did was beyond the law. He killed my father—just as surely as if he had put a bullet through him. I was just a boy, going to Groton, when he ran away with my mother. I didn't know the story, nor the name of the man, until my father told me—the day he died.

'Some men can take a thing like that, and laugh it off, maybe. But it killed my father. It took ten years to do it—but it killed him in the end. It killed his self-respect first, ruined his health, ruined his career. I saw him die—and I swore I'd get the man who was responsible, Cole. I've been looking ever since.'

Cole looked down into the valley, too. 'And

now you have found him?'

Calico nodded. 'Now I've found him,' he said softly.

* * *

Saber was a patchwork spread, set in a hollow between stony ridges. Several of the outbuildings were of stone, roofed by *piñon* poles. It had been a goatherd's camp once, until the Gillis brothers had drifted into the valley. Rumor had it they had been on their way to Mexico, but had lagged in San Ramos long enough to get wind of the state of affairs at the Cross B. They bought some equipment in San Ramos, sent a man back over the trail for reinforcements, and added several additions to the goatherd's shack. Thus Saber was born—backed by guns and bidding for a place in the valley.

Cole and Calico came down a well-worn trail into the hollow and rounded the corrals that had once penned goats. A hundred yards to their left lay the bunkhouse. The main shack, sagging a little at the rear, like some watchful lobo sitting on its haunches, lay ahead.

A Saber rider poked his red head curiously out of the bunkhouse to look at them. Another rider was standing before a mirror tacked to the bunkhouse wall, stripped to the waist. He was shaving.

The redhead in the doorway cursed and ducked back inside. The man with the razor whirled and half crouched, one side of his hard face white with lather. Cole recognized him from the meeting at El Toro's—the rider called Monte.

Two men were seated on the veranda of the main house. Cole knew them both. The Gillis brothers!

He raised his right hand. 'This is a peaceful visit, Cash,' he called. 'Call your men off.'

Cash grinned. He had gotten up, a rawboned man with a sandy stubble that didn't show the gray in it—a hard man who didn't need to swagger to prove it.

'Glad you came up, kid,' he said. He raised his voice slightly. 'Red—hold that itchy trigger finger. Let's hear what they have to say.'

Tom Gillis had remained seated. He was holding a drink in his right hand—his left hand was bandaged! Cole saw this, and his surprise sent a little shiver down his back.

Red stayed in the bunkhouse door, a silent, suspicious man, his hand on his gun. Monte wiped his face with a dirty towel hanging on a nail and picked up the gunbelt he had laid on the small bench beside the washbasin.

'I've come to bargain with you,' Cole began. 'Give us thirty days, and we'll pay you two dollars a head on every Cross B cow we drive through Horsethief Pass.'

Cash laughed outright. 'You're crazy, kid!'

Cole said grimly: 'We'll make it three dollars a head—payable after the herd is sold.'

'Ten dollars a head won't buy me off now,' Gillis snarled. 'I made yore brother an offer once—he turned it down. I don't have to bargain now, kid. The Cross B's beaten—and beaten men can't bargain!'

Cole watched Red. The Saber man had eased away from the bunkhouse door, half-turning his head as if listening to someone outside. A warning of danger crawled down Cole's back.

Barney had been right—there was no bargaining with Saber. But he had one last band to play—a worthless hand, but he must bluff it.

'I came to give you a chance, Cash—one last chance to settle this peacefully. The next time I come this way, I'll have backing.'

He couldn't clearly see the man who suddenly appeared in the bunkhouse doorway, pushing Red roughly aside. He heard Calico breathe: 'Look out, Cole!' and then Calico's horse jostled his as he spurred close.

A rifle spat wickedly in the stillness of the yard, and the echoes bounced back from the ridges. Calico gave a sharp grunt. Cole jerked around, his gun hard in his hand, as Calico's slug spun the rifleman against the door jamb and his second bullet dropped him limply across the threshold.

The rest of the scene became blurred. For

an instant, Cole recognized the man as Mike, the brawny kid he had humiliated in front of El Toro's, and later again in the Cross B yard.

Then Red was cutting loose at them, while Cash and Tom Gillis made a dive for the veranda floor.

Cole's slugs dropped Red. Monte made the corner of the bunkhouse and disappeared around it. From the veranda a Colt boomed angrily.

Cole swung his rearing horse. A slug burned across the animals haunch, sending it plunging wildly up the trail. Calico was bent a little over the saddle, leading by two lengths. Somewhere behind a rifle cracked once—the slug made a deadly whisper past Cole's ear. Then he and Calico were cutting around the long corrals which partially shielded them from the riflemen. When they hit the rise they were out of close range and the next shots were wide.

Cole followed Calico, his concerned gaze checking the other's doubled position. Calico was hurt! Cole cursed himself as a fool. He should have listened to Barney. Coming up here had gained him nothing, and only Calico's intervention had prevented Mike from getting even with him.

How badly was Calico hurt?

He urged the gray to a faster gallop and finally drew alongside Calico. They had come up out of a long swale between ridges, and

137

Cole noticed that the Bueno Padre River made its first bend here, to cut through Bueno Padre Canyon a quarter of a mile ahead.

'Calico,' he said sharply, laying a hand on the other's saddle. 'Pull up, feller!'

Calico nodded. His face was ashen under the dark tan. 'We left them something to remember us by, anyway,' he managed to grin.

'How bad are you?' Cole asked. 'Can you last to the Cross B?'

Calico smiled. 'Just a scratch, Cole. Grazed my ribs. I'm all right. You ride on ahead, though. Take the Bueno Padre trail in. I'll meet you—later—at the ranch.'

'Where are you headed?'

'Got business in San Ramos,' Calico answered. 'Something I should have attended to before—'

'You sure you're all right?' Cole asked anxiously.

'Go ahead,' Calico urged. 'I'm all right. I'll meet you later.' He waved briefly.

Cole watched him swing his horse away. He didn't believe Calico. The man was hurt—badly hurt. But Calico was headed out on private business—to kill a man.

Slowly Cole cut around and rode for the Bueno Padre trail.

138

CHAPTER FIFTEEN

Charles Brister drank straight from the bottle. He was beyond all nicety of manner now. Fear gripped him with iron fingers and shook him till his insides quaked—and half a quart bottle of bonded Scotch had not perceptibly eased the gnawing dread in him. His thick lips slobbered as he set the bottle down.

The band of sunlight which came in through his window had strengthened as the morning wore on, and heat lay like a heavy punishing hand in his stuffy office. Brister's tie was awry, his dirty shirt collar loosened.

He had been deteriorating slowly, despite his pretenses at social veneer, before John Carlson had given him a glimpse into hell. Since yesterday Brister had dropped all pretenses. He was an animal, trapped by his own blunders—and he alternated between the decision to flee at once from this corner of Texas or to seek sanctuary behind the guns of Saber.

But he did nothing. He sat alone in his stifling room and tried to drink himself into a stupor. Ann had tried arguing with him, reminding him of the doctor's warning—but Brister knew of a surer death awaiting him and he had laughed in Ann's face.

He got up now and lurched to the window.

This was the tenth time he had done so. From here he could see the valley trail—this was the way Henry Carlson's boy would come, as he had threatened.

Amy Carlson! She had been a weak woman. However, she had had social position, and wealth in her own name, and he had been a struggling lawyer trying to get onto that first rung of the ladder of success. Amy had given him that rung, and he had gone up on her shoulders.

She had died two years after Ann was born. She had been a mouse of a woman, patient and resigned—but he knew that long before she died, she had regretted what she had done.

He turned away from the window. Blast Cash Gillis, anyway, he thought. If he hadn't sent for me, promised me this easy money.

He had met Cash in Avondale, as he had met many men. Cash had been representing some big ranch, he had said, which had horses to sell to the Army. And he, Brister, had connections among the top brass, so—

He knew now that Cash had sized him up, judged him correctly. A dollar was a dollar—and honesty was a thing apart—a thing pretended, part of the social veneer.

He slumped back in his chair, his big bulk creaking the seat. 'Got to get out of here,' he mumbled thickly. 'Make a new start—California!'

'Ann.' He cursed her silently. She had been

a millstone around his neck from the day she was born. He was tired of pretending. She was Amy's girl—soft and sheltered. She even looked like Amy.

He forgot that he had fostered her illusions; his fear made him blame everyone but himself. In that moment he hated her because he had to think of her, too—

He reached for the bottle and dragged it to his lips. Behind him, in a walnut bookcase, were his books—symbols of the profession he had fought to achieve, and that he had dishonored. His law school diploma, in its dark mahogany frame, hung from the wall. It had meant something long ago, but he had long since stopped thinking of that meaning.

The footsteps on the stairs were Ann's. He recognized them, light and definite—and habit made him lurch forward, spilling some of the amber whiskey down his shirt front. He pulled open a drawer, intending to hide the bottle . . .

Ann came in before he could get it out of sight.

She stood in the doorway, a basket under her right arm; and though he had never considered her beautiful, there was poise and a graciousness about her that not even the shock of the past days could erase. She closed the door gently and came to him, placing the Mexican basket on the desk.

'I brought coffee, and some lunch,' she said. She reached for the bottle, but he pushed her hand away with a violent gesture. 'Leave it!' he snarled. 'I don't want lunch. Now get out of here and leave me alone!'

Spots of red crept into her cheeks. She had taken his insults and his rudeness until she was at the breaking point. Inside her now, a barely understood temper shook her.

'Drink yourself to death if you want to!' she lashed out. 'I'll not bother you again! I'm packing up and going back to Avondale—to Aunt Evelyn's.'

'You should have gone six months ago!' he sneered. 'But you insisted on tagging along. I didn't want you. You're too soft for this country. You're just like your mother—too soft and too sheltered. You don't fit in here, and I don't want you! Now get out—*get out!*' he yelled.

Ann looked at him—this was her father, this slobbering, unkempt man who reeked of liquor. She shuddered.

'You've never said anything good of my mother, have you?' Ann said bitterly. 'Before I go, tell me one thing. The man who was in here yesterday—he said his name was John Carlson. What was he to Mother?'

The liquor was beginning to befuddle him now, breaking down his long-held inhibitions. Suddenly he felt like hurting Ann, hurting her as he used to hurt her mother. 'You want to know,' he sneered. 'Well, your mother was married to another man when she ran away

142

with me. His name was Henry Carlson. John Carlson is his son. And your half-brother, too.'

He had gotten through to her. He saw it in her stricken face. The devils were really prodding him now. 'I wanted your mother for her money, for her social position. With them I became a big-wig in Avondale, in state politics. I had connections, so I made money. Oh, not always honestly—but it was the money that mattered.

'The pretty clothes you wore, that house we lived in—I had paid for them. And after your mother died, I used her money to speculate. I did very well, until that railroad deal—'

Her white hand had flown to her throat, clutching it. She seemed fascinated by his eyes, watching his every expression. Seeing her suddenly so helpless before him gave him an intensely perverse sense of satisfaction. 'You didn't know, did you?' he mocked. 'You didn't know that your father was a swindler?'

'I think I did,' she whispered, leaning dejectedly against the bookcase. 'I guess I did know, but I just wouldn't believe it.'

He lurched erect, his heavy face beet red. The liquor was affecting his legs. He stumbled to the wall and tore down the diploma. 'Attorney Charles Brister.' He laughed drunkenly and threw the frame across the room, through the open window.

Ann's voice was now very cold. She straightened up and came to the desk. 'And a

143

drunken coward, too.'

He came to her, his fingers digging into her arms. 'Sure I ran from Avondale. Think I wanted to spend the rest of my life behind bars? Is a man a coward for that?'

She twisted her arm away from him contemptuously. Off balance, he stumbled and nearly fell. He caught himself on the chair, his head lolling foolishly. 'I've got to get to Saber. I've got to see Cash. He'll stop that crazy kid.' He was mumbling thickly and almost incoherently.

'You had better go to bed.' Ann told him. 'I'll see John Carlson—if he comes!'

Brister suddenly sat in the chair. 'No! He's out to kill me . . . *he'll kill me!*'

Ann merely repeated: 'I'll talk to him.'

Brister lifted his head, eagerly grasping her offer of help. 'You'll talk to him, Ann? Keep him away? Till I can see Cash? He promised me protection if I came here—promised me easy money. Just take care of any legal complications, he said. I was supposed to share in the Cross B, when Cash took it over—'

He rubbed his eyes with a sweaty palm. 'It was the only way to get back on my feet,' he was saying. 'Ann, I did it for you. I wanted you to keep on having the things you had back in Avondale.' All his words were slurred, and he kept shaking his head tiredly.

Ann's voice was scornful. 'You did it for me? All that lying and cheating—for me!' She came to him. 'Get to bed! I'll try to talk to my brother when he comes!'

'Six months of waiting, Ann,' he mumbled dejectedly. 'Waiting for Cash to break the Cross B. But it's over now. Tomorrow night Buck Gaines and the town boys will raid the Triple A. When they're through there, Pedro Aragon will smash the Cross B for us!' He laughed heavily. 'Do you hear—the Aragons will do the job for us! They'll smash the Barretts, what's left of them—'

Ann shook him. 'Do you know what you're saying?'

'Aragon's north range, tomorrow night,' he slobbered. 'And I get a share of it, when Saber takes over.'

She pushed him away, straightening up. 'No! I won't stand for it! What you did in Avondale, I didn't know. I shut my ears to the rumors. I didn't *want* to believe. Why you came here, I hadn't guessed. I came because I thought it was my duty—a daughter's duty to her father.' She laughed shortly and contemptuously. 'But this you won't do. This is murder! And I'll stop it even if I have to go to Don Pedro with the story—'

At this, Brister came out of his chair, his head suddenly clear of fumes. 'You fool! Isn't it enough that it was for you that I came here? You want to ruin everything now—'

Ann strode to the door. 'Maybe it's not too late,' she flung back at him, 'to save everything!'

He reached her as she was turning the knob. His heavy hands, cruelly digging into her arms, spun her around. The sudden realization of what Cash Gillis would do, once he found out where the leak had come from, drove him insane.

'You're not going out!' he panted. 'You're not going to stop me—'

She shoved him away and tried again for the door. He hit her with his clenched fist, knocking her against the wall. 'No!' he screamed. 'No!' Again and again he hammered at her until she slowly slumped to the floor. He stood over her, gasping, his eyes wild with fear.

'Got to get out of here!' he wheezed. 'Got to go—' He fumbled at the door. 'Buck will know what to do . . .'

*   *   *

Bull Harkness stared at the wild-eyed, heavy man who had stumbled through the batwings. He was alone in the saloon, except for Slim Keegle, who was nursing a bad boil on his neck with copious draughts of red-eye.

Brister pounded on the bar. 'Where's Buck?'

Harkness scowled. He had never cottoned to Cash Gillis' argument that some day they would need a front man, a man who knew legal loopholes. Bull was like Buck in this respect—he knew only the use of force. He hadn't liked it when Cash had brought Brister in on the deal. His feelings had not changed with familiarity.

'Buck's out,' he growled. 'Quit pounding that bar before you disturb Keegle.'

'I've got to see Buck!' Brister insisted thickly. 'I've got to get to Saber—'

Harkness leaned over the counter. He had been able to smell the Scotch on Brister's lips when the man had come through the door. 'You're drunk!' he said contemptuously. 'Go back home and sleep it off!'

'You blasted flunky!' Brister snarled. 'I've got to get to Saber. My daughter knows about tomorrow night! She wants to go to the Aragons with the story!'

Bull reached across the bar and grabbed Brister's shirt front. 'You told her?'

Brister tried to squirm free. His shirt tore, leaving the cloth in the other's hairy hand. Bull raised his voice. 'Slim—come here a minnit!'

Slim came up to them, his hand on his gun. He was a thin-lipped, straw-haired hardcase who took orders from Harkness and Gaines.

'Now tell it slow—and tell it straight!' Bull rasped. 'How'd she find out?'

Brister shrank away from the gun that slid into Keegle's hand. 'I didn't mean to,' he said shakily. 'I had been drinking—'

Bull nodded slowly as he finished. He

147

looked at Keegle and shrugged. 'You did the right thing, Charley,' he said softly. 'Slim will go along with you. You and your gal will be better off up at Saber. Until everything's over with, anyway.'

Brister said: 'Sure—that's the best way. Cash will understand. Won't he, Bull?'

Bull nodded. 'Sure. Cash will understand!'

* * *

Calico slid out of the saddle. He looped the reins around his arm, knowing that if his mount drifted away from him he'd never get back. He sank to his knees in the shade of the gnarled *piñon*. His breath was sharp and his side was on fire. He was beginning to feel lightheaded.

His hands fumbled at the strap holding his canteen. He had to stay on his feet. He had a job to do in San Ramos. Over and over in his mind the thought repeated itself. *He had a job to do in San Ramos.*

The water was warm, but it took the parched and cottony feeling from his mouth. He took a long swallow and rested, his eyes closed. When he opened them again, he looked down a brush-spotted slope to a faint ribbon of trail that wound away among the foothills of the Pinnacles.

He had ridden in a circle. He knew that now. He had left Cole up by the Bueno Padre.

But in three hours he had lost his way. The road below must be the Saber trail to town.

His eyes were blurred. His side felt wet and sticky, and he felt around inside his shirt to the bullet hole under his ribs. He winced at the pain.

His horse moved restlessly, pulling him off balance. He lurched to his knees and caught at the stirrups and, with his fading strength pulled himself up.

Three riders came into view on the trail below.

He tried to focus. The heat waves blurred the riders. Calico rubbed his eyes. 'God,' he said simply, thankfully. One of the riders was Charley Brister!

He wiped his bloody hand on his trousers, and hope gave him strength. He pulled himself up, inch by inch, into the saddle. The animal snorted at the sudden hard pull of the reins.

'Just take me down, boy,' Calico whispered. 'That's all I ask—'

Brister saw him first. He was riding a length ahead of both Ann and Slim at Keegle's orders, and he recognized the rider cutting down the slope directly in front of them. He yanked back on his reins, a wild cry breaking from him. The startled animal almost sat back on its haunches.

Keegle spurred up quickly, momentarily diverted by Brister's move. By the time he saw Calico and went for his gun, it was too late.

Calico's drawn Army Colt slammed heavily in the hot, hemmed-in stillness of the hills.

The slug kicked Keegle out of the saddle. He fell limply in the path of Ann's horse and the rearing animal threw the girl. She fell on her hands and knees and cried sharply as her twisted wrist sent pains shooting up her arm.

Brister was cowering in the saddle, watching the dying man ride close. 'No!' he cried wildly. 'Don't shoot—you wouldn't shoot—in cold blood!'

Calico was bent over his saddle. His face was ashen, drawn. 'Yes, Brister—I can.'

Charley's eyes rolled. 'No!' He kicked the animal's sides, and the startled horse lunged away. Calico's gun cracked heavily. Brister stiffened. He straightened up in saddle, very tall, and then Calico fired again.

Brister swayed slowly to one side. His cayuse was still running, gathering speed, as he fell . . .

Calico watched him. He didn't see Ann, he didn't even seem aware of the girl crouched on the trail, her bruised face white and shaken.

He was very tired. Slowly he felt the gun slip out of his fingers, but he didn't care. He was through with it. He put both his hands around the pommel and his head came down on them. In his ears was a far away pounding, like surf on the beach . . .

Ann's voice finally penetrated to his consciousness. She had regained her saddle and had ridden beside him. Her voice was low and understanding.

'John—I know why. I know why, John.'

He tried to smile. He couldn't see her very well, but he thought that here was his half-sister. This girl his sister! He had never thought of her in that way. Now he'd never know her . . .

He said: 'Glad—you understand—'

Her hand was on his brow, cool and soft. 'Can you hang on for a while longer?' she asked quickly. 'Until we reach the Cross B?'

'I'll try,' he told her.

But he didn't make it. He was dead when Ann Brister rode into the Cross B ranchyard, leading his horse with the body draped across the saddle.

CHAPTER SIXTEEN

The Bueno Padre brawled its way down from the Pinnacles, slicing through the soft sandstone cliffs that barred its way to the Rio Grande. It twisted and turned on its way, making false starts here and there, and later, abandoning these tentative channels, left them to dry and whiten in the pitiless glare of the border sun.

Cole Barrett came down into one of these washes with the noon sun punishing him with its murderous heat. He let the gray drink thirstily in a small sandy puddle under the cutbank while he took a long swallow from his own canteen.

With every passing mile he had doubted the wisdom of his split with Calico. The man had been badly hurt. Decency would have required him to remain with the strange man who had hired out to the Cross B at a time when every hand was quitting. But he knew Calico had not wanted him along—that Calico preferred to go about his business alone. For this reason Cole had consented to the separation.

Yet it had been for Cole Barrett that Calico had risked his life—that he had taken Mike's bullet. Cole shrugged off his self-condemnation. Calico wanted it this way, he argued. And then, for a brief moment, his thoughts speculated on the man Calico wanted to kill, and curiously he thought of Charley Brister. He remembered Ann's hasty excuse when he had expressed the desire to see her father.

What had brought Charley Brister to this corner of Texas? The question occurred to him again, bringing faint puzzlement. Brister had been a big man in Avondale—a man with influence, wealth and prestige. Such a man was not likely to throw all that aside to make a new start as a lawyer in a small border town.

He shrugged thoughtfully, remembering that his own family had quit an old homestead to come here. But they had some excuse. Texas, in these years of carpet-bag rule, was a hard place for a former Confederate sympathizer to live in. Some of Martha's bitterness, her implacable hatred, he attributed to the turmoil prevalent throughout the state.

'But one can't go on hating forever,' he thought harshly. 'It's got to end somewhere. The war's over. What's done is done!'

Marcus and Barney and Martha—and only his father had wanted him back. Only his father had forgiven him. And a small measure of regret came to Cole then; regret at the wasted years. A sorrow for the years that had been, when Jay and Bill and Mom were alive, when he was a kid on the Brazos ranch, taking a pole down to the 'hole' for the big catfish. Days that would never come again.

He swung the gray away from the puddle and squared his shoulders against the burning heat. He'd make it up to Martha. He'd try to make her understand—try to make her forget. This was a family affair, this matter of the Cross B, after all. What was the use of fighting for it, if the family came apart at the seams, if sister was against brother in the final showdown?

For it was open war between Saber and the Cross B now. The ride up to the Gillis ranch had at least smoked this out into the open.

And his bluff, flung at Cash Gillis, had not been entirely without backing. There was a chance to break Saber yet—if old Pedro Aragon could be made to see who was behind the raids on his cattle, the deviltry that was deliberately being stirred up in the valley. This was the Cross B's last chance . . .

He had crossed the wash and was cutting through a clump of dwarf pine when he saw the rider. Clad in jeans and blue chambray shirt, leading a loaded pack horse. Even through the heat haze and the distance separating them, Cole recognized his sister. She was riding fast, and she seemed to know where she was going.

Cole reined back to the protection of the pine clump. Unbelieving, he watched her ride past, less than a hundred yards away. There was a stiff and determined set to her shoulders, and from the looks of the pack animal's burden, Martha Barrett had made good her promise. She was leaving the Cross B for good!

He waited until she went out of sight around a sandstone shoulder; then he swung the tired gray around. With mixed emotions he followed her, wondering where Martha would be headed—and inside of himself, knowing.

*   *   *

Martha rode at a fast pace, disregarding the deadly heat. Sweat darkened the shirt under her armpits, made little rills down her cheeks.

The glare of the washes made her squint—but she rode at a steady clip, glad at last to be free.

Barney had not tried to stop her. He had come to the veranda while Hank helped her fasten her personal baggage to the pack animal. He had watched her, the strange, quizzical smile on his broad face that made her guess that he knew.

She had flung her challenge to Cole and she couldn't back down. But all that morning she had been undecided—and until she got into saddle and rode out under the adobe arch that had been home now for three years, she had still been unsure of herself. Waiting in the yard for Hank to tighten the last knot on the pack animal, she had even hoped that Barney would say something—something that would hold her. But Barney had said nothing to her—not even good-bye.

She had left the Cross B that way, without looking back even—and she knew she would never return. Now that her decision was made, there was a lightness in her. She was going home! She was going to the man she loved—her father's deadliest enemy. And she was going freely, willingly, turning her back on her brothers, on her father, on her home.

She rode with head high, and as the end of her journey neared, a soft light came into her eyes. The light Cole had seen the first night he had spent at the Cross B.

It was midafternoon when Martha rode

down into the hollow that sheltered Saber. The ring of her horse's shod hoofs on the stony trail brought a rider in a quick run around the bunkhouse, a rifle in his hands. She rode past him, pulling up before the sagging ranchhouse.

Cash Gillis opened the door and looked out. He said: 'It's Martha.' He stepped aside as his brother came out and ran quickly down the stairs to meet her.

He was grinning, and the strong cut of his lips caught at her, reassuring her with their strength. She swung down into his arms, and he kissed her roughly, ran his hands through her hair, and then fisted her nose gently.

'You made up yore mind, I see,' he said. And there was a gentleness in Tom Gillis' voice that brought a scowl to Cash's face. He had not fancied a woman coming to Saber. This was a rough outfit, and women had no place in it. But Tom wanted this Barrett girl, and Tom could be mighty stubborn in things like this. He remembered another time and another girl—in Natchez, it had been . . .

He shifted his chaw of tobacco and curved a juicy stream over the veranda. 'Better come inside, 'fore the sun gits both of yuh,' he advised gruffly.

Tom took Martha's hand. 'Might as well see what home's like,' he grinned. He turned to the scowling Saber rider with the ready rifle. 'Take care of Miss Barrett's animals. Turn them loose in the corral with the others. And bring her things inside, Jeff.'

He went up the steps with her. 'Yore brother and that gun-handy drifter, Calico, paid us a visit this morning,' he explained. 'They killed Mike and Red Berringer. But I think Calico left with a slug in his hide . . .'

'Too bad it wasn't my brother,' Martha said uncompromisingly. 'Paw and Barney would have given up before this, if he hadn't come along.'

'He'll get his,' Cash assured her quietly, eyeing her. 'After tomorrow night the Cross B will be through. All we'll have to do is ride down and take it over.' He looked across to Tom and nodded, understanding some things more clearly now.

'She'll be the sole surviving Barrett—looks like,' he said, grinning. 'What's left of the place will be hers—all legal and nice-like, eh?'

Tom was looking at Martha, his eyes sober. 'You sure you want it this way?'

She raised her eyes to him, and in that moment she irrevocably shut herself from her people and smothered the last shreds of doubt. 'Yes,' she answered harshly. 'This is the way I want it!'

*　　　*　　　*

Cole crawled back from his position of concealment on the slope overlooking the hollow. He got into the saddle and turned the gray away, keeping to a thin screen of pines that clothed the shallow ravine. Not until he was well along on the trail to San Ramos did he allow himself to think.

He had seen his sister ride boldly into Saber, and into the arms of Tom Gillis! The revelation had the impact of a slug, and it left him numb, and for a long time he rode without definite plan, like a man hit a low blow and left temporarily helpless.

The devil with it! he thought dismally. I'm getting out of here. I should never have come back!

But through the confused thoughts an eager, broken voice came. His father's voice: '*You'll fight, Cole . . .*'

They had had their differences, he and his father—but they were more than eight years gone. His father had wanted him back—and Barney would follow his lead. He pulled himself out of the morass of his hurt, and anger began to shape up in him, to burn harshly in his throat.

He was staying. He was seeing this thing through if he had to drag Barney with him—if he had to do it alone, with all the Barretts against him. He scarcely knew this broken-down Cross B, but he had come to value it—and he wasn't going to stand by and see it go by default!

He leaned forward in the saddle and urged

the gray to greater speed. He wanted to see Barney. He wanted his brother to ride with him to call on Don Pedro . . .

The sun slid down behind the Conquistadores, and the purple shadows marched in ghostly step across the valley. A bright star, yellow and big as a man's fist, hung in the eastern sky, so low a rider could stand in his stirrups and pluck it. A soft, cool breeze stirred and rustled in the swiftly falling dark, and it brought to the hard-riding man the sound of gunfire, faint and intermittent, yet chilling in its implication.

He was still a half-mile from the Cross, riding along a coulee bottom whose white sand gleamed faintly in the dusk. But he could place the gunfire ahead of him, and for a brief, incredulous moment Cole imagined that Saber had beaten him to the Cross B—that it was the Gillis crowd besieging his father's ranch.

He slowed the almost spent gray to a walk, and finally dismounted. Colt in hand, he eased forward, keeping to the cover of the coulee that grew more shallow as it neared the outbuildings of the former de Gama hacienda.

The night helped. Plus the fact that not one of the besiegers were expecting a caller from the rear!

Several yards ahead a rifle spat wickedly, its red flare momentarily outlining a swarthy face. A man cursed in Spanish, and thirty yards to the left another man answered him. Cole recognized the authority in this man's tone, and he smiled thinly. This was Manuel—old Pedro Aragon's firebrand foreman!

He waited, judging the strength of the attackers. There were about a half-dozen of them, and they were playing it safe. The answering fire from the house was sporadic. Cole counted three guns, and he tried to place the defenders. Barney. Hank. Who was the other? Calico? Had Calico made it to the Cross B?

The cursing rifleman in the darkness ahead slammed another shot into the house. Colt palmed his .45. He came up behind the man and made him out, a stocky shadow lying on his stomach behind a split-rail fence that had once housed de Gama hogs. The man sensed his step and turned his head, his voice questioning. 'Manuel?'

Cole hit him with the side of his Colt. The sound didn't carry ten feet. The man rolled over and lay still.

Cole eased silently away, heading in the direction of Manuel's voice. Unsuspecting, the Triple A foreman was giving orders to close in.

He was standing, a tall shadow at the corner of the first adobe outbuilding, when Cole came up behind him. He came up fast, jamming his Colt into the other's back. 'Shut up and listen!' he growled in Manuel's ear. 'Now drop your Colt!'

Manuel obeyed. He was stiff in the

160

darkness. He didn't try to turn.

Cole slid an exploring hand over the man's body and found a knife in a neck sheath. He tossed it into the darkness. Manuel wore only one gun, and it was now at his feet. Cole's probing toe found it; he scuffed it away.

'Now you'll call this fandango off!' Cole ordered grimly. 'If you want to live to see daylight, call them off. Give them orders to get into saddle and ride home. Savvy?'

He felt Manuel's body quiver. But the Triple A foreman nodded. '*Si.*' The word seemed to stick in his throat. 'I have no choice, *señor.*'

'None!' Cole agreed.

Manuel's voice raised. He rasped orders sharply. From the darkness came surprised, questioning calls. But Manuel, under the prodding of the gun in his back, lashed them with a voice that brooked no opposition. 'Go back to the rancho!' he ordered bitingly. 'I will follow later.'

One by one the men obeyed. The sound of their riding faded into the night.

Manuel's voice was bitter. 'And now, *señor*?'

'You'll come with me,' Cole said. He gave the foreman a shove in the direction of the ranchhouse.

'*Barney!*' His voice cracked in the stillness. 'Barney—it's me. Cole. I'm coming in. Hold your fire!'

Somehow, in the darkness filling the yard,

161

he thought he heard a girl cry out. Then Barney's voice, clear and strong, answered: 'Come ahead, Cole.'

CHAPTER SEVENTEEN

Ann Brister was standing in the center of the big living room when Cole entered, pushing a sullen Manuel before him. He noticed her first of all, saw the bruises that marred her face, the powder marks smudging her chin. She was holding his father's Winchester, and her left wrist was tightly bandaged.

He saw her first, and he forgot the others— Hank and Barney—waiting silently beyond. He went to her, not knowing how or why she was here, but suddenly aware of her need of him. She went into his arms, and only then did she break down—and her voice was broken and incoherent . . .

'Cole— Cole. He's dead— Calico's dead— my brother—'

He held her tightly, sensing her need of his strength. Hank and Barney looked on wordlessly.

She repeated herself, as if she had to make herself understand, as if she had need to spill her grief this way. 'He killed my father—and he's dead, Cole!'

'She rode in this afternoon,' Barney

162

volunteered. 'Right after Martha left. Calico was dead in his saddle. She said she wanted to wait here for you—had something to tell you.' He shrugged and turned his gaze to Manuel, standing arrogantly against the wall. 'Then this joker showed up with a half-dozen Triple A vaqueros and began shooting up the place . . .'

Cole guided Ann to a chair. He eased her into it and took the rifle from her hands and placed it down on the floor. He wiped her face with his handkerchief, his eyes narrowing at the darkening bruises on her cheeks and jaw.

'Calico killed your father?' he asked.

She nodded. She lay back in the high-backed chair and closed her eyes. 'I need you,' she whispered. 'I haven't any place to go now.'

His hand closed over hers. 'This is home,' he said. 'If you'll honor me by staying?'

She smiled weakly and opened her eyes. 'The old fortune-teller was right,' she whispered softly. 'She said I'd meet my destiny fifteen hundred miles from Avondale—and he would be the young second lieutenant I had met that night.'

Barney cleared his throat. 'I don't know what happened up at Saber,' he said. 'But Martha left. I didn't try to stop her.'

Cole shrugged. 'You were right about Cash,' he admitted. 'He wouldn't bargain.'

Barney shot a look at Manuel. 'What do we do with this joker, kid?'

'Take him back,' Cole answered. 'Tonight. I

163

want to see Don Pedro. He's our last hope, Barney.'

Ann took hold of Cole's arm. 'The raid!' she said sharply. 'I almost forgot. The raid on Aragon's north range, tomorrow night.'

Cole looked down at her. 'What is it, Ann? Who's going to raid the Triple A?'

She told him the story, the long and shameful story of her father and his connection with Saber. And of Buck Gaines' projected raid tomorrow night, of her father's decision to flee to Saber, and the meeting on the trail with Calico.

Cole listened quietly, only now understanding Calico's mission.

From the hallway a weak voice called: 'Cole! Cole—my boy—'

Cole tamed. Barney nodded at the look in his eyes. 'Yeah. Paw came out of it. He's been waiting for you, kid.'

Cole went into his father's bedroom. Marcus tried to sit up, but Cole eased him back on his pillow. 'Take it easy, Paw,' he said gently. 'You've had your day. Sit back and listen.'

He told Marcus what had happened, of his ride up to Saber, and his reception there. But he omitted mention of Martha—there was hurt enough here.

Marcus nodded tiredly. 'You'll win out, son. You've got the will—you'll fight—'

Cole smiled. 'I've been bluffing this far,

164

Paw. But thanks to Ann, we hold the joker now. Old Pedro will have to listen. And if the town crowd pull that raid tomorrow, they're through. They don't know it yet but that raid is going to break Saber!'

He stood up. 'Ann and Hank will stay with you, Paw. Barney and I are riding to the Triple A.'

'*Vaya con Dios*,' Marcus whispered.

*   *   *

A sullen Manuel rode a length ahead of them, down the long trail to the Triple A. The gibbous moon ran ghostly fingers through the sage and the *bosque* of the Salt, but the three men rode silently, creaking saddle leather muffled by hoofs in the sand. Each rode with his thoughts—Manuel's feeding his anger, building on his humiliation until he had to check the hot tide within him.

Barney was thinking back to the boy that had been Cole, to life on the Brazos ranch, before the war had intervened and irrevocably changed everything.

Cole sensed his brother's dark mood. 'I saw Martha,' he said bluntly. 'She rode to Saber. To Tom Gillis.'

Barney didn't look up.

Cole said sharply: 'You knew?'

'Since the first,' Barney replied. 'It took the fight out of me, kid. I couldn't see any sense in holding on, after that.'

Cole said: 'I hope she's happy, Barney.' And he meant it.

They came to the willow-shadowed road to the Aragon hacienda just before midnight. They rode in boldly, hemming Manuel in between them, so he wouldn't make a break for it.

The Aragon place was similar to the old De Gama hacienda—but even at night Cole could see the difference. There was an air of order here, of neatness and of proud possession, and it gave him a glimpse into what the Cross B could become.

They rode into the yard, and at their order Manuel called out. There was a stir in the dark buildings on their left. A dozen men, some only partially clad, tumbled out into the yard, guns gleaming in the moonlight.

They ringed Cole and Barney in a tight, questioning circle.

Lights came on in the main house. Finally the door opened to the wide veranda and a tall, gaunt-framed man in a wine-colored robe stepped forth. Behind him a frightened man-servant peered, holding a three pronged candelabra aloft.

Don Pedro's voice was irritated. 'Who comes to disturb us at this hour of the night?'

Manuel sneered. 'The Barretts. They wish a word with you, Don Pedro. They say they have a story to tell. But if I were you I would have

166

none of them.

'I'll heed my own counsel!' Don Pedro interrupted coldly. 'Who ordered you to attack the Cross B? I have heard of the outrage. Your men came back earlier. Tell me, whose idea was it?'

'Mine,' Manuel replied sullenly.

'You take things too often into your own hands, Manuel. Some day I will call you to an accounting!'

There was movement behind the master of the Aragon acres. Juanita stepped out to stand beside her father on the veranda. A satin cloak draped her slim, night-clad figure, and in the moonlight her hair shone with a thousand golden glints.

Admiration was in her eyes as she looked at Cole. 'The last Barrett,' she said to her father. 'He is the one I spoke to you about.'

Don Pedro turned to her. 'I'll have no daughter of mine interfering,' he began angrily. 'Get back into the house—'

She ignored him. She walked down the stairs, smiling at Cole. 'Welcome, *Señor* Barrett, to the home of my father.'

Jealousy surged in a red, murderous tide through Manuel. For seven years he had ridden with this girl, daughter of his *patrone*— and kept his desire leashed. She had taunted him and teased him, as she did with every man she captivated—but he had held himself, knowing that to overstep his bounds would result in quick dismissal, if not worse.

He had watched her with other men, and always, he could control the acid of his jealousy. But the look in her eyes tonight was almost wanton—she was welcoming this gringo as she had welcomed no man.

He swung down out of the saddle and shoved her aside, and turned to face Cole. 'He is a Barrett!' he snarled. 'An enemy. Have we forgotten who has been raiding our cattle, destroying our property? Have we become so blind—'

'Fool!' Juanita interrupted. 'Go to your quarters. You have made enough trouble tonight—'

'It isn't finished!' Manuel whirled, snatched a Colt from the hands of a vaquero standing by. 'I have waited long enough!' he cried harshly. 'I shall show you—'

'*Manuel!*' Don Pedro's voice lashed out at him. 'Have you lost your mind? These men have come in peace. As my guests they have a right to be heard . . .'

But Manuel was beyond reason. 'I shall show you, Juanita,' he whispered, 'that thees Barrett is no better than the others. I shall give him his chance. See—I drop this gun into my holster. We are even now, *señor*. And I shall not wait.'

Behind him the men scattered silently. The stars looked down on this scene, old and wise with other memories.

168

'Thees time,' Manuel snarled, 'thees time, I give the orders. *See?*' He lunged sidewise, drawing swiftly.

Cole's Colt bucked heavily. Manuel's bullet touched his hat in brief salute. Slowly, with stark amazement on his dark face, Manuel stared up at Cole. His gun hand dropped first, letting his weapon slide down to the ground. Then his knees bent and he collapsed . . .

Juanita looked with stunned fascination. Cole slid his Colt into his holster. Barney stared with impassive face.

'I'm sorry he forced me to it,' Cole said levelly.

Don Pedro nodded. He seemed suddenly tired—a gaunt, raw-boned man with deep lines in his brown face. His temples were whiter than the rest of his hair.

'You had to defend yourself, *señor*. But maybe Manuel thought he was doing right. Tell me, why are you here?'

'Because, like yourself, I am tired of this trouble between us, Don Pedro,' Cole answered. 'There is no reason for this enmity between the Cross B and you.'

'The raids on my cattle—' Don Pedro began stiffly.

'—are the work of Saber,' Cole finished. 'And the riff-raff that hang out in the Lone Star in town.'

Don Pedro shook his head. 'You can prove this, *señor*?'

Cole nodded. 'I can prove it, Don Pedro.'

Juanita interjected quickly: 'Listen to him, Father. He does not speak lightly—'

'I will hear what you have to say,' Don Pedro acceded. 'Come inside.' He turned to the watching figures. 'Chico! Miguel! Pablo! See that Manuel's body is taken care of. We'll have services in the morning—'

*   *   *

The room they sat in was massive. The low ceilings were ribbed by huge timbers, hewn from oak that had been cut and hauled a thousand miles in Mexico. Artfully woven tapestries hung from the cool walls, framed portraits looked down at Cole—stern Castilian ancestors, cloaked and knighted. Over the organ hung Juanita's portrait. The artist had caught her warm tones and her temper—and managed also to convey, not flagrantly, the willfulness of this girl who ruled in a household usually dominated by its men.

Don Pedro caught Cole's glance and offered information. 'My daughter was painted by Pilano, in Madrid, two years ago, *Señor* Barrett.'

Barney sat stiffly. He felt uneasy here. He was a rough man, rough in speech and ways, and he felt alien in this big, cultured room.

Cole nodded. 'A beautiful painting, Don Pedro,' he agreed. 'But you are doubly lucky.

For you have more than the painting—you have your daughter.'

Don Pedro smiled. 'You have a way with words, *Señor* Barrett—'

'And a way with men,' Juanita added, and her eyes, luminous in the candlelight, spoke more than she said. Don Pedro noticed this and frowned.

'The raids have been getting out of hand, *Señor* Barrett,' he said bluntly. 'Manuel was sure the Cross B was behind them. My son, Julio—' He made a weary gesture with his hands, 'Julio thought so, too. He's disappeared. I confess I am frantic. My wife has taken to her bed. Julio was not one to stay away these many nights of his own accord.'

'Concerning your son I know nothing,' Cole replied. 'But consider these facts, Don Pedro. Before I came into the valley, the Cross B had less than a half-dozen riders. My brother Barney had all of them, up in the Benches, trying to get a bunch of our cattle together for a drive to the northern beef markets. Our range was wide open and unprotected—easy to cross unnoticed at night from Saber. Easy to raid clear onto your range.'

'But why?' asked Don Pedro. 'Why risk that long drive for a few cattle, when yours are closer?'

'Because cattle, your cattle, is not the prize,' Cole answered grimly. 'The Cross B is what they're after. Don't you see, Don Pedro? If they could make you certain that the Cross was your enemy, if they goaded you hard enough, you'd take your men and ride. You'd wipe out the Cross B—and then they'd take over. And if ever an investigation was started from Houston, you would be the man the law would question. You would be the one on trial, not Saber!'

Don Pedro stroked his shaven chin. 'I see, *señor*. And yet—how can I know this is not just what you are planning? To get me turned against Saber—to get my help against the Gillis brothers?'

Cole smiled. 'That is just what I hoped for, Don Pedro. I'm going to prove that Saber has been raiding you—Saber and the town gang that hang out in the Lone Star Saloon. Tomorrow night, if my information is correct, Buck Gaines will lead a raid on your northern range. And they will leave behind evidence implicating the Cross B. I swear that this is true.'

Don Pedro frowned. He turned and walked to the organ, his shadow long in the candlelighted room. 'There has been too much of killing already,' he murmured. 'But if this is true—'

'My brother and I are here—in your hands,' Cole pointed out. 'Hold us here. Let us ride as hostages with you to your northern range. And if the raid does not come off, you have us in your power. You may do with us as you will,

172

Don Pedro.'

Aragon turned. 'You are sure of yourself, *Señor* Barrett.'

Cole thought of Ann, waiting for him at the Cross B. He was risking his and Barney's life, the entire future of the ranch, on her information. 'I am sure,' he said.

'Then you will remain here tonight,' Don Pedro ordered. 'As my guests—we will say.'

Cole looked at Barney, a slow smile lengthening on his lips.

CHAPTER EIGHTEEN

The mesa of the crazy grandee who had blown to bits both himself and the trail leading up to its summit cast its long and bulky shadow over the Triple A's northern range. Against the star-studded sky Cole fancied he could make out the turreted roof of the old nobleman's house, as aloof as the planets above. Inaccessible now, brooding over the valley, stained with violence . . .

This was where the whispers began, the stories told in the hovels of the Mexican quarter—the gilded legend of old Don Miguel. For it was here that Miguel's ghost came forth, to swing his deadly sword . . .

Cole turned his gaze to the men around him. Barney was stolidly unmoving, waiting

173

beside his mount. Don Pedro walked restlessly. The others, eighteen strong, lay scattered and silent among the shadows.

Below their position several hundred of Aragon's best beeves were bedded down for the night. The cattle were strung around the little pond that caught the reflection of the million stars. The moon had not come up yet.

This was the crucial moment—this moment of waiting. He had played his hand on a girl's story—and the Cross B's fate hung in the balance on what happened this night.

There was movement among the shadowy figures beyond. Don Pedro stopped his restless pacing. Barney came to Cole's side. 'This is it, kid,' he said softly.

Down the far slope a band of horsemen, ghostly in the night, were beginning to fan out. A gun broke the trembling quiet—a flat, violent report that brought the cattle lumbering to their feet. Frightened lows went up in the dark.

The raiders fanned out now, spurring forward into a run. The gunflares began to wink like angry fireflies, and the reports smashed across the basin and came back multiplied by the hemming hills. The cattle were up and milling now, and suddenly they turned and began to run.

Don Pedro got into the saddle. The others followed, clustering around the patrician boss of Aragon acres. 'This night we put an end to it!' he cried, and spurred down the slope.

Cole and Barney rode together. With the others they hit the raiders in a flank attack that turned them back upon themselves, set them to yelling confused and angry questions.

The attack became a rout. Above the roar of stampeding hoofs the guns of Aragon's vaqueros and the cries of wounded men made a medley—a mad disorder of shouts and shots. But the Aragon riders had the advantage of surprise—and of attack. In the darkness they picked their targets, and the fleeing men had little chance. One man got clear, and he was riding doubled up over his saddle as he faded into the night.

The moon came up, strengthening the light of the stars. Cole rode slowly toward Don Pedro, who had dismounted beside a fallen horse.

The old Don was kneeling beside a body, and something in the set of his shoulders touched Cole, brought him down quickly beside the other.

The face of the man Don Pedro held was young, brown and faintly resembled Juanita's except that the man's hair was raven black and his chin had less determination. It was a thin, sensitive face. Without being told Cole knew this was Julio, Don Pedro's missing boy.

He was dead. He had been brutally beaten and then shot in the back and left to die. On his charro jacket, pinned there, was a scrap of paper.

Cole scraped a match for Don Pedro to read by. A few scrawled words, intended for Pedro Aragon.

> *Here's your son. If you want more, come to the Cross B.*

It was signed in bold scrawl: *Marcus Barrett.*

Buck Gaines lay sprawled just beyond his dead horse. He had died instantly, a bullet through his head, and his Colt was still in his fist.

'He had my boy across his saddle,' Don Pedro whispered. It seemed an effort for him to talk. The veins in his neck were bulging. 'Julio was still alive when I got here. He died in my arms.'

Cole said nothing. Barney came up, wiping a bloody face, holding his neckerchief to a furrow across his cheek.

'Chico!' Aragon turned to one of the silent men at his back. 'Take Julio home!'

He held up the body and helped Chico pull it across his saddle front. *'Vaya con Dios, hijo,'* he said wearily.

The big black moved restlessly as he got into saddle. 'We ride to Saber!' he said shortly. 'Tonight!'

They hit Saber at dawn!

One by one the stars faded from the sky—and a saffron light spread like an unfolding fan in the east, drivng the shadows from this dry and stony land.

They had come to Saber in the false light, a hard-riding company spurred by the night's grim tragedy. Cole lined his sights on the bunkhouse window, and his rifle crack sounded reveille in the morning stillness.

For long moments that crisp report bounced off the rocky walls, fading finally into distance.

'Cash!' Cole's voice called down to the ranchhouse. I've come back, Cash. With Don Pedro!'

The silence flowed back over the sound of his voice. And for a moment Cole thought they had arrived too late! Then the door opened in the ranchhouse and a woman stepped out to the porch. A girl in Levis and blue shirt, with her hair loose on her shoulders. With a carbine in her hands.

Martha Barrett!

'Come down, Cole!' she invited harshly. 'Come down and show yourself!'

Then Tom Gillis appeared beside her—a tall, blond man with a bandaged left hand. 'Come and get us!' he sang out.

Barney's shot chipped wood two inches from the man's head. Tom lifted his Colt and fired back; then he pulled Martha back inside. And as if this was a signal, rifles spat their answering defiance from the bunkhouse.

Don Pedro glanced at Cole's white face.

Then he waved his hand in signal to his waiting men.

There was but one window in the bunkhouse, facing them—and they laid a barrage into it and into the house, while others crept down under the covering fire. Cole moved down with them. He wanted Tom Gillis! He kept remembering the tall man in armor—the man who had almost killed his father—who had killed his brother Bill. The man who had jerked his left hand in to his body, in a hurt gesture, that night at the Cross B, when Cole had fired at him.

Miguel's ghost! This was the man who had terrorized the valley, wearing a suit of Spanish armor and brandishing a fine Toledo blade.

He went down in a zigzagging run, a Colt in his hand. He heard Barney call after him, but he was intent on making the house. A bullet kicked up dirt under his boot. Another came so close that he heard the deadly whisper of it.

Then Martha came out of the house. She came out ahead of Tom Gillis, covering him defiantly. He hesitated a moment, then broke for the corral just beyond the house.

Cole stopped. Martha had swung toward him. He saw her lift her carbine, but he couldn't shoot. Somewhere behind him he heard a shout, but it seemed far away. He tried to step back, and Martha's finger tightened on the trigger. And in that awful moment he remembered most clearly her eyes—wide and without reason. Then the rifle went off and she was falling, a look of hurt surprise on her face . . . a look he would always remember.

He ran to her. Barney came up and they both knelt beside Martha. Around them the firing was sporadic, fading.

He looked up at Barney and let his glance drop to the other's Colt. Barney shook his head. 'No—I didn't do it, Cole.' And Cole nodded, glad it had not been Barney. Someone else, but not Barney—and he would never ask who.

Don Pedro came up to them. 'One got away,' he said grimly.

Cole straightened. 'Tom Gillis! The man who came out with my sister . . .'

The old Don nodded. 'He's mounted on one of the best horses in the valley, *señor*—the golden palomino.'

'Your black'—Cole asked grimly—'I'd like to ride him.'

Don Pedro waved a hand up the slope where he had left his mount. 'You're welcome to him, *Señor* Barrett. I have always fancied Negrito as the fastest horse in this part of Texas. He is yours.'

'I'll bring him back,' Cole said bleakly, 'or I won't come back . . .'

*   *   *

It was a wild chase that led down from the

Pinnacles, across the rolling foothills, past the upper Salt, and across Aragon's northern ranges. Horse against horse—golden palomino against midnight black—barb Arabian against barb Arabian.

Tom Gillis had a half-mile start, and he kept it—but he didn't lengthen his lead. He ran that golden horse to exhaustion. But he couldn't gain on that powerful black. And toward the end of the day the palomino began to fade . . .

They had come across the entire valley, taking slope and bad country at a killing pace. Gillis had been heading for the old trail through the Conquistadores. But he knew he wouldn't make it through these savage hills without being overtaken.

Suddenly he doubled back and headed straight for the old mesa atop which perched the mad grandee's castle.

Cole came upon the spent palomino at the base of the cliff. A low sandstone ridge came to meet the mesa here, falling off abruptly as though some great axe had chopped down, dividing the ridge from the mesa proper.

Cole left the black alongside the palomino. Part way up the sandstone ridge a Colt spat angrily, the slug ricocheting off a rock close by. Cole made a run for the cliff. The near vertical wall protected him from the man above. Slowly he worked around until he saw footholds; then he began to climb.

It was a dangerous job. Occasionally he

glimpsed Tom Gillis above him, but never long enough for a shot. Sometimes Tom's gun flared down, chipping rock by Cole's face.

Cole conserved his shells. The sun smashed down on them, baking the ridge. Sweat caked Cole's shirt, ran down his legs. He reached the top of the ridge and exposed himself cautiously.

What he saw froze him—made him forget the gun in his hand.

Tom Gillis was making a run for the ridge where it sheared off from the main mesa wall. He was fast for a big man, amazingly light on his feet. And he didn't stop at the edge. He jumped.

And only then did Cole see what Tom Gillis was after. A small ledge on the mesa side, clinging like a shelf to the sheer wall. And a trail that wound up through a fissure, out of sight, to the top . . .

Gillis made it. He landed lightly and Cole cut down on him, belatedly. The Saber man twisted and fell back against the rock wall, and his Colt jarred out of his hand. It dropped with metallic clatter out of sight in the crevice.

Cole had a brief glimpse of Tom's triumphant, corded face. Then the man made the fissure and squirmed out of sight.

Cole measured the jump with his eyes. About fifteen feet. Not too great a distance, but the drop was more than a hundred feet to rock-piled debris below. He wiped the sweat

181

from his eyes and thrust his Colt into his waistband. He unbuckled his belt and let belt and holster drop.

He made the jump. He misjudged his distance and landed way up on the ledge and brought up against the cliff wall with a jar that almost unbalanced him. He felt his Colt slip free and he twisted and made a desperate grab for it. But it slipped through his fingers, hit the edge of the ledge and went spinning down to join Tom Gillis' weapon on the rocks below.

Cole stood up. His hair was in his eyes and he thrust it back, feeling his wet palm across his forehead. He didn't need a gun. He needed only his hands . . .

*　　　*　　　*

Mesa Grande castle shouldered its battlemented defiance to the setting sun. Built of hewn rock, brought piece by piece up the narrow trail by toiling natives, it squatted in lonely splendor, haunted only by turkey buzzard and fierce-eyed hawk.

Nothing had been disturbed since the nobleman owner had died—only a film of dust had taken occupancy.

Up the wide stone stairs a man raced. Behind him came Cole Barrett, breathing heavily. Gillis passed through the silent, open doors and vanished, and a moment later Cole plunged inside.

The abrupt change from blazing sunlight to semi-darkness brought Cole up short. He closed his eyes, and in that moment he heard Tom's harsh, ragged laughter.

'This is the end of the long trail, Cole,' Gillis panted. 'I'm through running. This is where it all started—long ago—when I first discovered the way up here.'

Cole massaged his eyes. He could see Tom Gillis now, across the big room that once upon a time had been Don Miguel's trophy hall. Armor was set on pedestals, swords and lances crossed on the tapestried walls. Priceless rugs, paintings . . . much of the wealth and the heritage of old Spain was displayed here, out of time, out of another era.

But Cole saw only Tom Gillis, waiting for him across the dusty hall. And a grim smile formed on his lips. 'This is where I pay you for Bill—and for the others,' he grated. He reached up on the near wall, where crossed sabers hung, and wrenched them free. Turning, he sent one skidding across the floor to Tom Gillis.

Tom picked it up, hefted it. 'An older score, Cole,' he snarled. 'An old score from Missionary Ridge . . .'

It was a strange duel, there in the dust of the years. Saber on saber, clanging in the brooding silence.

A strange duel—and in the end Tom Gillis lost. By a fluke—by fate, if you will.

He had forced Cole back against the wall and was beating down Cole's guard. Cole went down to one knee before Tom's savage assault. And Gillis, sure of himself now, swung high in an overhead cut that would have severed Cole's head from his shoulders.

His saber caught briefly in the wall tapestry. Just enough to twist his stroke and tilt him off balance. And Cole came up in a lunge, his saber sliding under Tom Gillis' ribs . . .

Tom dropped his weapon. Both his hands came down to grip Cole's blade. His eyes rolled, and a choked gurgle bubbled from his lips. Then he fell, dragging his body free of Cole's blade.

The long shadows of late afternoon were marching across the valley as Cole paused on the edge of the mesa, where the trail down to the valley began. Far off in the distance the mission bells of San Ramos were calling—a peaceful sound.

Calling him home—and to Ann Brister.